Alice zigzagged between her parents and then in and out of the surf. She imitated some sandpipers chasing waves. "I hope I find a junonia this year," she said. "Or at least an alphabet cone or an angel wing."

"They're all beautiful to me," said her mother. She had a faraway look about her, a dreaminess.

Alice thought it would be nice if everyone's heads—except her own—had small windows built into them and she could see what was going on inside their brains. She imagined that her father was thinking about what they would have for dinner. She imagined that her mother was thinking about world peace or the glory of the ocean. Right now, Alice was thinking that she'd feel much better if she found a rare shell.

JUNONIA

KEVIN HENKES

GREENWILLOW BOOKS
An Imprint of HarperCollins*Publishers*

Junonia
Copyright © 2011 by Kevin Henkes
First published in 2011 in hardcover; first paperback edition, 2012.

The text of this book is set in 12-point Century Schoolbook BT.
This book is printed on acid-free paper.
Book design by Kevin Henkes

Library of Congress Cataloging-in-Publication Data
Henkes, Kevin.
Junonia / by Kevin Henkes.
p. cm.
"Greenwillow Books."
Summary: The week of her tenth birthday, Alice and her parents go to Sanibel Island, Florida, just as they do every year, but this time some of the people who are always there are missing and some new people have come, which unsettles Alice, who wants things to be exactly the same as they always are.
ISBN 978-0-06-196417-6 (trade bdg.) — ISBN 978-0-06-196418-3 (lib. bdg.)
ISBN 978-0-06-196419-0 (pbk.)
[1. Shells—Fiction. 2. Seashore—Fiction. 3. Change—Fiction.
4. Sanibel Island (Fla.)—Fiction.] I. Title.
PZ7.H389Jun 2011   [Fic]—dc22   2010010346

12 13 14 15 16 SCP 10 9 8 7 6 5 4 3 2 1
First Edition

Greenwillow Books

For Laura, Will, Clara, Susan, Anne, Jane, and Bob—
thinking of, and remembering, Florida

Fan Scallop

Jingle

Shark's Eye

Coquina

Conch

Auger

Clam

Cockle

Sailor's Ear

Alphabet Cone

Angel Wing

Tulip

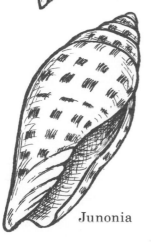

Lace Murex

Whelk

SOME

FLORIDA

SEASHELLS

Junonia

Kitten's Paw

CHAPTER 1

When Alice Rice and her parents were halfway across the bridge, Alice felt strange. Her breath caught high in her chest and she became light-headed. It seemed as though there wasn't enough air in the car.

"Look," said Alice's mother from the front seat. "It's beautiful."

"As always," said Alice's father. He was driving. He slowed the silver rental car. "What do you think, Alice?"

The sun was blazing. The water—beneath and beyond them—glinted wildly. Seconds earlier, Alice had been thinking that the surface of the water was like glossy, peaked blue-green icing sprinkled with truckloads of sugar. Now, she had to remind herself to breathe. She was dizzy and slightly afraid. Her hands were clenched. What was wrong? This had never happened to her before. She'd always loved the bridge, loved the feeling of being suspended, like a bird, between the mainland and the island.

"Alice?"

The sensation passed as quickly as it had come. "Beautiful," Alice finally said, relieved. "I wonder who'll see the first dolphin this year."

"I don't know," said Alice's father, "but there's the first pelican." He pointed. To the left of the car and not much higher glided a big, drab, knobby bird.

"They look prehistoric to me," said Alice's mother.

Alice concentrated entirely on the pelican. The bird was so odd and silly looking, a mysterious, mesmerizing wonder. Alice reached out, pressing her palms flat against the half-opened window. She'd seen pelicans before, every year that she had been here, but when you see something only once a year it's always new, as if you're seeing it for the first time. Everything is new here, she thought. New and exciting.

The pelican plunged out of sight, and Alice's mind drifted back to the feeling she'd had. She was somewhat superstitious and wondered if the feeling meant that something bad was going to happen. She tried to shake the thought out of her head. She was hoping that this would be the best trip she'd ever had. They would be celebrating her birthday on this trip. In a few days. This, alone, wasn't unusual—her birthday always came during their annual vacation—but what made this year special was that this would be her most important birthday yet. Ten. Double digits.

"Heron to the right," her mother announced.

"Ibis!" said her father. "Straightaway."

"Seagull!" said Alice, sinking into a warm, cozy happiness. "Over there. And over there and over there and over there . . ." Her voice was bubbling with laughter.

Minutes later, they were on land, the island. This was Alice's tenth trip to Sanibel Island in Florida. Her family always came in February when it was cold and dreary back home in Wisconsin. Just this morning they'd left behind three inches of new-fallen snow, icy winds, and a leaden sky.

Alice was thinking that the sky in Florida—so blue and transparent—was better than the sky in Wisconsin. "Blue, bluer, bluest," Alice whispered.

The palm trees, the lacy pines, the bright unfamiliar flowers, and then the town unrolled before her.

Everything seemed illuminated, and glazed or made of glass.

Alice was an only child, as were her parents. All four of her grandparents were dead. Her family was small, but in Florida she pretended that her family was big. She pretended that the people who stayed in the neighboring cottages on the beach, the people who returned at the same time each year as she and her parents did, were part of her family.

The Wishmeiers and their grandchildren; Helen Blair; ancient Mr. Barden; and Alice's mother's college friend, Kate. They were Alice's big family. They didn't exactly look like they all belonged together the way some families did, but Alice didn't mind.

Alice had a pale, watchful face. She had straight brown hair and brown eyes and a brown spot the size and shape of an apple seed near the corner of her mouth. The spot was a mole, but Alice hated the word *mole* and referred to it as a speck. She hated the speck, too, and had decided she'd have it removed when she was old enough to make decisions like that without her parents' permission. Her parents repeatedly told her that it was called a beauty mark and that it made her extra pretty, and that one of her great-grandmothers had paid to have fake beauty marks, which she'd kept in a little tin box on her dresser and wore when she wanted to be fancy.

Neither of Alice's parents had moles on their faces, but they did have straight brown hair. Her father was an architect and his name was Tom. Her mother worked in an art gallery and her name was Pam. Alice thought her parents' names suited them. Tom, the name, was short and solid, like her father. And Pam, spelled backward, was map. Her mother always seemed to have the answers, seemed to know what to do. She knew the way, and not just when driving a car or hiking.

Alice liked her last name, Rice, because it rhymed with nice, and she took this as a good sign.

Alice liked her first name most of the time. She didn't like it when her father called her Alice in Wonderland, which he rarely did any longer. He did still call her Pudding, which she didn't mind as long as none of her friends heard him. Pudding was short for Alice Rice Pudding, which he found hilarious.

Alice had given up wanting a brother or sister. "Out of the question," her father would say. "I'm too old," her mother would add. Alice thought that a brother would have made her family complete, especially a brother named Eric, because Eric and Rice have the exact same letters. Back home in Wisconsin, Alice had a stuffed polar bear and a purple betta fish called Eric. And she'd already named their rental car Eric, too.

Before Alice knew it, her father was steering Eric off the road onto a narrow driveway of crushed seashells.

The crunch beneath the tires was familiar. They stopped briefly at the tiny office to check in and get the keys. Then they drove toward the beach between two rows of low, pastel-colored cottages. They pulled up to number two—the cottage Alice and her parents stayed in every year. It was painted cotton-candy pink.

"Here we are, Pudding," said Alice's father.

And they were.

And Alice was filled with joy.

CHAPTER 2

Before they unpacked the car and settled into the cottage, they always took a first look at the ocean from what Alice considered her beach. Alice ran ahead, reaching the shoreline before her parents. A shiver of excitement coursed through her. She knew that it was the Gulf of Mexico that lay before her, but to Alice it was simply the ocean or the sea, because the word *gulf* seemed too small for something so big. On the apron of shiny sand, Alice kicked off her shoes, then inched forward to test the water. It was cold, so she jumped back, staying just beyond the water's grasp. Looking from left to right, up and down, there were only two things: sky and sea. Alice blinked her eyes and gulped the air as if she could draw the whole blue world inside her and keep it forever.

Her parents caught up with her. Her mother grabbed Alice's right hand. Her father placed his hand on Alice's left shoulder. The three of them stood in silence, dwarfed.

It felt to Alice that her brain was splitting apart into pieces, each piece telling her to do something different from the others. One piece was saying: Stay with your parents. Another was saying: Hunt for shells. Another: Unpack your bag. Still another: See who else is here.

Alice's eyes swept over the beach, searching for any great shells that might have washed ashore and not yet been discovered. Then, suddenly, she broke free from her parents, turned around, bent down, snatched her shoes, and headed back toward the cottage. "I'm going to see who's here," she called. She was loose jointed, and although she felt awkward much of the time, she often appeared graceful. She swung her arms in smooth half circles; her legs moved like ribbons.

The brilliant orange gladiolus in the vase on the screened porch of cottage number seven meant that the Wishmeiers had arrived. Alice leaped up the steps and knocked on the door.

A deep, friendly voice drifted out to greet her. "Is that my girl from Wisconsin?"

"Yes, it is," Alice replied.

Mr. Wishmeier appeared before her and threw open the flimsy door. Alice entered the screened porch and, after a moment's hesitation, leaned into him for a hug.

Mrs. Wishmeier was waiting with a hug of her own for Alice.

Early on, years ago, Alice had been afraid of the Wishmeiers. They'd seemed big, stern, and formal, like concrete statues in a public park. But, over time, they'd changed in Alice's eyes. They'd become warm, jolly, and easy to be with. Sometimes Alice pretended that they were her grandparents.

Mr. Wishmeier was a retired English professor; Mrs. Wishmeier was a retired elementary school principal. They were from Michigan. They both had short-cropped silvery blond hair and shiny pink skin. They were tidy in appearance—no jeans or T-shirts for them. When they strolled the beach they wore matching wide-brimmed straw hats, and Mr. Wishmeier used a walking stick, the handle of which was carved to look like the head of a bear, a bear inlaid with red glass eyes that Alice imagined to be real rubies.

"Are Colin, Chad, and Heather here yet?" asked Alice, nearly breathless. They were the Wishmeiers' grandchildren; their father was Mr. and Mrs. Wishmeier's son. Colin and Chad, twins, and Heather were older than Alice, but they never dismissed or ignored her, and they treated her with genuine kindness and not a trace of condescension. They were the older siblings she'd never had.

"I'm sad to say they're not coming this year," said Mrs. Wishmeier.

Mr. Wishmeier nodded and offered an apologetic, tight-lipped smile. "Too much schoolwork to be missed. Colin and Chad started high school this fall and Heather's in eighth grade now." His square shoulders drooped, becoming uneven.

"A young, unfriendly couple with a noisy baby are staying in their cottage," said Mrs. Wishmeier. The tip of her tongue flashed out and in. "It breaks my heart."

"Oh, Judy," said Mr. Wishmeier, "that's harsh and unfair. It's not their fault our kids aren't here. Don't misdirect blame."

Once, last year, Alice had overheard Mr. Wishmeier call his wife a troublemaker, and Alice had ballooned with pleasure at this glimpse of a private moment.

Mrs. Wishmeier tossed her hand and her head and sniffed dramatically. "Well, we'll have more time to spend with you," she told Alice, her voice softening.

"Oh," was all Alice managed to say. Disappointment seeped into her. Her face was a sad moon. Her big family was shrinking.

Suddenly, from outside, a familiar, quavery, gentle voice called, "Look who I found." The voice belonged to Mr. Barden, Booth Barden, the oldest person Alice had ever met. He was in his nineties and stayed in the cottage closest to the ocean. He had found Alice's parents and was standing between them outside the screened porch, curved over his cane, gripping it tightly. "Is that nice little girl in there?"

Alice and the Wishmeiers went out and there were proper greetings all around.

Mr. Barden lowered his glasses and studied Alice, smiling. Then, as if he were trying to wipe food off her face, he brushed at her speck with his thumb. Normally Alice would have despised whoever was doing this (it had happened before), but because it was sweet Mr. Barden with his crinkled, papery hand, he was forgiven, despite her embarrassment.

Mr. Barden had a smooth, dappled head with the most delicate wisps of white hair sticking out from behind his ears. His nose and chin were sharp, his fingers bony. His eyes were sunken into lavender hollows and were so pale and milky it was difficult to say what color they were. His features were a combination of hard and soft, and Alice couldn't decide if he reminded her more of a baby bird or a wizened old one.

Alice blurted out the disappointing news that Colin, Chad, and Heather would not be coming.

"Oh, that's too bad," said Alice's mother.

"Sorry, Pudding," her father said quietly.

"I already knew that," said Mr. Barden.

Then the five adults talked on and on, and Alice felt misunderstood. How could they discuss traffic on the island and the weather at a time like this?

"I'm going to unpack," said Alice flatly. "Good-bye and see you later," she added, trying to be polite, trying to hide the sulkiness that was rising up in her.

Alice withdrew and marched away, with her parents close behind her.

When Alice's father unlocked the door to the pink cottage and Alice stepped inside, she brightened up instantly. Sunlight streamed through the windows. The walls of the main room and of each smaller room were paneled with honey-colored wood, once highly polished, now scrubbed or rubbed dull in places. The floors and low ceilings were wooden, too, very knotty, and each year Alice felt as if she were entering an enchanted house from a fairy tale—the interior of a tree or an enormous worn-out shoe or a giant nutshell. The many knots were benevolent eyes, keeping watch day and night.

All of the cottages were named for seashells. Alice's cottage was named Scallop. A small oval plaque engraved with elegant lettering hung above the front door on the outside, making it official.

"Hello, Scallop," said Alice, twirling around. "It's so good to see you again."

CHAPTER 3

Alice went right to work. She neatly stacked her clothes in the dresser. She lined up her shoes and sandals under the window. She hung her jacket on the peg in the closet. And then she flopped down on the bed, sinking into the soft mattress.

The sun-bleached bedspread was printed with a pattern of a seaside Chinese village. Alice ran her finger over rooftops and archways, over billowy swarms of butterflies and blossom-covered trees. Like a sailing ship, her finger traced over waves that reached up toward the clouds and swirls of mist.

Here and there, the bedspread was threadbare, but Alice hoped it would never be replaced. She often fell asleep imagining that she was part of the village, wandering the twisting streets among the butterflies, collecting armfuls of fallen blossoms.

Alice turned onto her back. With her eyes half closed, she stretched her arms and legs as far and wide as possible, covering the bed. She was thinking that she was a butterfly. She was wiggling her fingers and toes—fluttering her wings—when she heard a sharp rapping at the front door.

It was the Wishmeiers. "Message from the office," Mrs. Wishmeier said through the screen. "More bad news. Helen Blair can't make it. She's snowed in in New York. Biggest storm in years, apparently."

Alice and her parents flanked the door. Mr. Wishmeier

opened the door a crack and carefully slipped something into Alice's hand. It was a hollow sea urchin, purplish, light as paper. "For you," he said. Mrs. Wishmeier had already moved on, spreading the news. Mr. Wishmeier chuckled sadly, wrinkling his forehead, and stepped quickly in the direction of his wife.

Alice heaved a deep, miserable sigh. A new black cloud was putting its stamp on the day.

"I know," said her father.

"Maybe she'll rebook her ticket and come tomorrow or the next day," said her mother.

"I really wanted to see her," said Alice. The urchin was beautiful, but it didn't change how she felt. "This is going to be my worst trip to Florida ever."

"Not true," said her mother.

"Let's see the urchin," said her father.

She handed it over, thinking that Helen Blair would have had something wonderful to say about the urchin, something that no one else would say. And she would have said it with such unwavering attention that Alice would have felt as if she were the only other person alive.

Helen Blair always stayed in the cottage next to the Rices'. She was an artist from New York City. Every year she'd have wonderful gifts for Alice's birthday, often including something she'd made herself. Last year she'd given Alice a small bird she'd sculpted out of clay. It sat on Alice's dresser at home, next to her jewelry box and her jar of her best seashells.

Helen Blair played tiddlywinks and jacks with Alice, she did card tricks, she made the most spectacular sand sculptures, and she'd taught Alice a game called Sweet or Sour. To play, you wave and smile at passersby. If they wave or smile back, they're sweet. If not, they're sour.

Alice preferred coming across sour people, because

Helen would roll her eyes and lift her head to the side with a flourish, saying, in her fluty voice, something like, "Sour. Absolutely, positively sour."

Helen was probably as old as Mr. and Mrs. Wishmeier, but she seemed much younger. Alice thought of her as a friend more than an adult.

"Let's take a walk on the beach," said Alice's mother.

"Grab a bag for shells," said her father. "I feel lucky."

Alice didn't feel lucky. Not the slightest bit.

They'd rambled down the beach for quite a distance and were coming back.

"We're empty-handed," said Alice.

"Empty-handed?" said her father. "Speak for your-self. This bag weighs a ton."

"But it's filled with common shells, and they don't count." Alice zigzagged between her parents and then in and out of the surf. She imitated some sandpipers chasing waves. "I hope I find a junonia this year," she said. "Or at least an alphabet cone or an angel wing."

"They're all beautiful to me," said her mother. She had a faraway look about her, a dreaminess.

Alice thought it would be nice if everyone's heads— except her own—had small windows built into them and she could see what was going on inside their brains. She imagined that her father was thinking about what they would have for dinner. She imagined that her mother was thinking about world peace or the glory of the ocean. Right now, Alice was thinking that she'd feel much better if she found a rare shell.

The water was darkening. The patches of tall grass, the palm trees, and even her parents' faces were softened by the sinking sun. Clouds, like shredded rags, were scattered across the sky. Up and down the beach, people gathered in groups to watch the sunset.

Just as the sun dropped from sight, Alice had a

realization. It struck her suddenly that if Helen Blair wasn't coming, someone else would be staying in her cottage. There were so many awful possibilities to consider, and so Alice tried to drive the subject from her mind. But it was there nonetheless, bothersome, like something lodged between her teeth.

After sunset, they went out for dinner and grocery shopping. As the evening wore on, Alice's eyelids grew heavy. When Alice and her parents returned to the beach, Helen Blair's cottage was dark and empty. Alice felt a mingling of sadness and relief—and exhaustion. She couldn't wait to get into bed. Her arms and legs seemed to be bound with weights as she moved from the car to the porch. Climbing the few steps was a chore.

Once inside, Alice's parents tugged off her clothes and maneuvered her into her thin nightgown as if they were undressing and dressing a doll. Quickly, her body was turning itself off. Her parents gently tucked her in. Within minutes Alice was asleep, breathing steadily beneath the twisting streets of the Chinese village, her hands curled at her chin like unusual, smooth pink seashells.

CHAPTER 4

Alice didn't believe that God was an old man in flowing robes with a white beard and a temper to beware of. An old man who didn't come to the rescue during wars or when kids got picked on at school. Lying in bed on the first morning of her vacation, Alice decided her perfect, personal god was female. She would live in the ocean because water covered most of the earth, and her name would be Junonia because a junonia was such a rare shell, the one Alice coveted more than any other.

It had taken Alice a moment to remember where she was when she woke up. And after she had, a range of emotions passed through her—from happiness about being in Florida to lingering disappointment about Helen Blair and Colin, Chad, and Heather.

Alice heard the muffled voices of her parents coming from the kitchen and she could smell coffee, but she remained in bed a few minutes longer, considering Junonia, as the small room filled and brightened with sunshine.

Junonia would be old, but not too old, beautiful, but not too beautiful. She would be kind and wise and gentle.

All of a sudden Alice erupted from bed, before the morning hurried by without her. She reminded herself that her mother's friend Kate would be arriving today. Aunt Kate, Alice sometimes called her.

Oh, Junonia, Alice said in her head, will today be a better day?

The imagined voice replied, Yes, yes, indeed it will.

In the kitchen the sunlight cast an unexpected watery pattern on the table and on part of one wall. We're under the sea, thought Alice, smiling.

Because this was vacation, there were doughnuts for breakfast, and milk in one of the thick cobalt blue glasses from the tall, tilting cupboard. The glasses made the milk look different, and taste different, too.

Alice was working on her second doughnut when her mother's cell phone rang. At first Alice didn't pay attention because the doughnut and the milk tasted so good, but she took notice when she heard her mother say, "Kate! Oh, Kate, you're still coming, aren't you?"

Alice's listening sharpened. Her half-eaten doughnut

was poised in the air near her opened mouth. Powdered sugar freckled her lips; a clump of powdered sugar fell onto her lap.

"Is he nice?" continued her mother. "You did? Oh, good. What? How old? Well, Alice was feeling lonely. . . . Okay. We'll see you later. Bye."

"What?" said Alice.

"Wow," said her mother.

"What's up?" asked Alice's father.

"Kate has a new boyfriend with a daughter. They're all coming. Kate called the office, and she reserved Helen Blair's cottage."

"That Kate," said Alice's father. "She's always good for a surprise."

"The girl is named Mallory," Alice's mother told them. "She's six." She paused. "Kate sounds happy. Oh, and his name is Ted."

Alice blinked back tears.

Colin, Chad, and Heather. Gone.

Helen Blair. Gone.

Kate. Aunt Kate. Not gone, but nearly as awful. Coming with a boyfriend and his daughter.

Kate was the closest thing Alice had to a relative. It would be different this year. Every other year, Kate had stayed with Alice's family in their pink cottage, sleeping on the sofa in the living room. Every other year, Alice had had Kate to herself; she hadn't had to share her with anyone except her parents.

The doughnut turned to dirt in Alice's mouth. The playful pattern of sunlight on the wall, which had elevated her mood just minutes earlier, now seemed frenzied, as if it were laughing at her misfortune. She swallowed hard. She licked her lips, then pensively gnawed her lower one.

Alice's parents exchanged a look, and Alice could

tell that they were speaking in the secret, silent language of parents.

Questions raced through Alice's mind: When will they get here? How long will they stay? Will I get to spend any time alone with Kate?

The sun was suddenly obstructed and the room became noticeably darker, and seemed, too, to be thinking of what to do or say next.

Alice's father had placed his hands flat on the table. He wiggled his fingers methodically, as if he could sense words, the proper response, rising up through the painted surface. He suggested that, after breakfast, he and Alice go to the shell shop in town.

Her father's suggestion confused Alice. She loved going to the shell shop, but it was well known that he did not. He was making the offer, most likely, because he also thought this new development would not be a good one and he was trying to lift her spirits.

"Okay," Alice said quietly.

"I have a feeling," said her mother, "that everything will turn out beautifully."

"It usually does, Pudding," said her father.

Alice didn't get anything at the shell shop, no shells, that is. She'd greedily eyed the junonias that lined a glass case, looking like chocolate-sprinkled croissants in a bakery. There were buckets of banded tulips and alphabet cones, too. Shells of all kinds. Some from Florida and some from places more exotic.

Her father followed her up and down the aisles. He remained silent, but Alice remembered his comments from years past: "Why pay for something you can find on the beach? The shells seem fake here, all clean and polished. Like plastic."

Last February, when Alice had whined and pressed on and said, "But they have shells I've never found.

Rare ones," he'd responded by saying, "But if you buy them, it's cheating."

Recalling these remarks (particularly the one about cheating) was enough of a deterrent. She tightened her lips and picked out a small wooden frame to which one could attach little shells. She bought a bottle of glue, too, both with her own money.

"Why didn't you get a shell?" he asked.

She couldn't find the right words to cobble together an explanation; she shrugged.

Driving back to the cottage, Alice was angry at her father, Kate, the world. She felt the pull of something beyond her control, something unseen and unfair. Just to make noise, she said, "I named the car Eric."

"Good idea," said her father. "Eric is a fine car." He tapped the steering wheel. "Eric is a gem."

Despite herself, she was already forgiving him. Her father's jolly voice had broken the dark spell she was under, but only for a moment. She bounced lightly on the seat and hoped he'd say something funny or tell a joke. When he didn't, she sat upright and asked, "Do you know anyone named Mallory?"

"No," he said. "But I will soon."

CHAPTER 5

Alice waited for Kate. She ran up the driveway to the main road and back, repeatedly, until her new flip-flops hurt her feet. Then she sat on the front steps with her arms crossed, knocking her knees together gently and clucking her tongue against the roof of her mouth. She decided that this kind of waiting—waiting for something good and bad tangled together—should be given its own special name.

Alice imagined that Kate's phone call during

breakfast had been part of an elaborate prank, yet to be revealed. Although she knew it was next to impossible, she still wished that Kate would show up alone. No Mallory. No Ted. She closed her eyes and started counting to one hundred slowly, hoping that by doing so magic would be set into motion and Junonia would materialize and intervene. Alice's face was so tightly scrunched, spots and sunbursts pulsed across her eyelids.

She was at number seventy-three when she heard a car approaching. Her heart drummed in her chest. No matter how hard she tried, she couldn't keep her eyes shut.

"Kate!" Alice yelled. "Aunt Kate!" She raced to the car. Kate was sitting on the passenger side of the front seat. For a moment Alice blotted out the fact that there were two other people in the car with Kate. Alice opened the door before the engine had been turned off.

"You've grown three feet since the last time I saw you," Kate said, rising.

They hugged. Kate! thought Alice happily. Kate, Kate, Kate, Kate, Kate! When they broke their embrace, Alice's parents and Ted and Mallory had joined them. Introductions were made. And just like that, there were two new people in Alice's world, and her excitement evaporated into the swampy air.

Ted Rumbelow was a tall man with a bushy mustache and a slow, deep voice. His handshake was so firm Alice thought her fingers might break as he gripped them.

And Mallory. Mallory Rumbelow had a round face, round cheeks, round eyes, round knees, and a round nose. When Alice looked at her, she saw circles.

Mallory was clutching a limp doll made of pale blue corduroy, worn and dirty. The color matched her eyes perfectly. When she lowered her head and kissed her doll, Mallory's two yellow pigtails jiggled. One damp, loose ringlet clung to the skin above her left eyebrow like an upside-down question mark.

"Munchkey wants to see the ocean," were the first words Alice heard Mallory say. And that's how Alice learned the doll's name.

The group meandered to the beach together. Kate played with Alice's hair and held her hand part of the way. Alice could feel Mallory staring at her, but when she turned to look at her, Mallory either averted her eyes or covered her face with Munchkey.

On the sand, they took in the view, then formed a little knot. Alice's mother and Kate leaned into each other, whispering. Alice's father and Ted were laughing about something. Mallory stood on her father's foot, grasping his shirt with one hand, her other hand holding Munchkey. Alice was between her parents but felt disconnected. Invisible. She stepped away just a few feet from the group.

She watched the endless procession of long waves

rolling toward the shore. The crests were white and foamy. The hollows between the crests were deep, like trenches scooped out by a huge shovel. After a while, she saw the crests as strips of lace laid out on folds of steel blue cloth.

Alice turned back. When she was close enough to be heard, she asked Mallory, "Do you like the ocean?"

Mallory glanced up, then burrowed her face into her father's shirt.

Alice tried again. "Does Munchkey like the ocean?"

Mallory let go of her father's shirt and approached Alice cautiously. They walked slowly together along the tide line.

"Munchkey's mother went to sea in a pot, and she's been missing for weeks," Mallory said, her voice high and thin. "She might never come back."

Alice didn't know how to respond. There was a lengthy pause. Into their silence entered the squawk of a bird, snatches of the adults' conversations, the pounding of the waves. "*I* like the ocean," Alice finally said. "Aunt Kate—Kate—likes it, too."

"I think the ocean smells bad," said Mallory.

The warm breeze did carry a fishy smell, but to Alice it wasn't a bad smell, and it came and went lightly as the breeze quickened and lulled.

Mallory sniffed, jutting her head this way and that way. "I think it stinks," she said. She wrinkled her nose. "And Kate is not your aunt." Her eyes grew wide and became blank and shiny; she looked as if she was about to cry. She swung around and went back to her father, her pigtails bouncing. She pulled at his pants.

Alice frowned. A spark of annoyance flared within her chest. She remembered that her mother had said that Mallory was six years old. Alice realized how lucky she was to be nine, almost ten. Six seemed so young.

CHAPTER 6

Throughout the rest of the day—most of which was spent on the beach—Alice tried her best to get used to Ted and Mallory.

Ted seemed to know more about birds than most people did. He could tell the difference between a least sandpiper, a western sandpiper, and a spotted sandpiper. This impressed Alice. She'd always considered a sandpiper a sandpiper, nothing more. Ted cleared his throat often, and he hummed a lot, too—a low, melodious rumble. If Alice's father had done those exact things in those exact ways, she would have been embarrassed, but neither Mallory nor Kate seemed bothered by Ted's mannerisms. There was a smattering of moles on Ted's back and shoulders that reminded Alice constantly (and sadly) of her speck. However, she did like his bathing suit—it was printed with dogs wearing sunglasses.

When Ted put his arm around Kate's shoulders or rubbed sunscreen on her back, Alice could feel a storm well up inside her. She wanted to keep her distance from him, but she wanted to be near Kate.

Mallory was difficult for Alice to figure out. One minute she was shy and clingy, a barnacle on her father's leg, and the next minute she'd make some pronouncement with a hard face and a snippy voice: "I'm hot" or "The sun's in my eyes" or "I'm thirsty."

At one point in the afternoon, Mallory heaved

handfuls of sand into the air, laughing. There wasn't much wind, but enough that the sand drifted over the group. Alice felt the sand strike her legs. When Ted told Mallory to stop, she defiantly threw sand at him. He calmly got up off his towel, took Mallory by the hand, and led her away. Mallory pitched a fierce tantrum, stamping her feet and flailing her arms about.

Alice watched. She narrowed her eyes and craned her head with awakening interest. There was something about the ordeal she found exciting.

A few minutes later, Ted and Mallory came back. Mallory picked up Munchkey.

"We're going to the cottage for a while," Ted told them.

Mallory ground her heel into the sand and exclaimed furiously, between gasps, "Munchkey's *not* happy."

She didn't seem to be addressing anyone in particular. She wants the world to know, thought Alice.

Mallory repeated it as she departed, "Munchkey's *not* happy."

"Who is?" Kate said a moment later, lowering her sunglasses and rolling her eyes. She laughed helplessly.

Alice thought this was her first chance to be alone with Kate, but Kate stood and motioned for Alice's mother to follow her. "We'll be right back, sweetie," said Kate.

"Where are you going?"

"A short walk."

"Stay with me," said Alice's father, patting the towel beside him. His voice came from beneath the opened book that covered his face.

"I thought you were sleeping," said Alice.

He chuckled. "Through the wailing?"

Alice didn't respond. She settled next to her father on her mother's towel.

"What are you thinking?" The book remained on her father's face like a little tent.

It was a question he asked often. A question Alice usually didn't like to answer truthfully. She curled her lower lip. "Nothing."

Without looking up, Alice's father stretched out his hand, found hers, and pressed it gently. "Maybe you'll become friends. . . ." His voice trailed off.

Alice doubted it. She sat up. She felt thick and restless at the same time. She shifted about on the towel. Overhead, gulls circled in wide loops. Fixing her eyes on a single bird, Alice followed it until it intersected with another bird, and then she followed that one. She did this—from gull to gull—until her eyes smarted from staring up into the bright sky.

When Alice's mother and Kate returned from their walk, Alice had forgotten the gulls and was lost in thought about her birthday. She was building up a brilliant party in her mind. In her fantasy, a beautiful bakery cake would be delivered to the cottage on her special day. The cake would be tiered, five layers, similar to a fancy wedding cake. Two people would be needed to carry it—that's how big it would be. It would be frosted in sea blue and studded all over with shells made of spun sugar. Instead of candles, there would be ten sparklers stuck into the top layer of the cake like a bouquet of white, electric chrysanthemums.

"I need your help," Kate said to Alice as she plopped down next to her. "I've got a plan."

The cake vaporized instantly. "What?" said Alice.

Kate slid her sunglasses up onto the top of her head. She edged closer to Alice, lifted Alice's chin, and spoke to her in a confidential way. "Let's get Mallory interested in shells. She needs something to . . . something fun to think about and keep her occupied. And you're a shell expert. What do you say?"

"You'll do it with me?"

"Of course. We'll be a team."

"What about Ted?" asked Alice.

"Let's give Ted a break," said Kate.

"Okay," said Alice. "Just the two of us."

"Well," said Kate, "*three* of us. Don't forget Mallory."

"Oh, yeah," said Alice, laughing. "Duh."

"Another correction," said Kate, her expression worn and tender. "*Four*, not three. I'm sure Munchkey will be joining us."

CHAPTER 7

When Ted and Mallory came back to the beach, Mallory's eyes and cheeks were puffy and red. The circles that defined her face were more pronounced than ever. While Kate suggested looking for shells, Mallory hung her head, striking a tragic pose. She seemed to embody pure misery, and yet she took to the idea with a little coaxing.

"Ready?" asked Alice.

Mallory wove her fingers together and sighed.

"It'll be fun," said Alice.

"Okay," said Mallory, nodding.

Alice had gotten her shell guide and three plastic bags in which to collect their shells.

"Before we begin," said Alice, "I should show you what to look for." She flipped open her guide and explained which shells were common, which were considered good finds, and which were rare treasures. Alice's chest inflated with authority as she spoke. "The junonia is the best. Every year I hope I find one and I never do."

"I bet *I* will," said Mallory, perking up. "That's what I'll look for—a junonia." She dragged out the word *junonia*, pausing for a beat between each syllable as if it were four words.

"It's harder than you think," said Alice, trying to keep her voice from becoming sharp with irritation.

"I'm a good finder," said Mallory. "Let's go."

Alice started off, Mallory was at her heels, and Kate followed close behind, carrying Munchkey and the guide. They left Ted with Alice's parents.

Some shells seemed to be everywhere—clamshells and scallops and sailor's ears. Alice barely noticed them, but Mallory was scooping them up as though they were quarters and nickels and dimes scattered at their feet. "This is easy," she said.

"You should be more picky," Alice said quietly.

"What?" said Mallory.

"Oh, nothing."

When Alice found a lightning whelk—the first interesting thing she spotted—she held it out for Mallory to see. She told her its name, then said, "It's not perfect. It's chipped at the bottom, but it's pretty good." Alice had several lightning whelks at home. Bigger ones and ones in better shape. She offered it to Mallory. "Here," said Alice. "You can have it."

Mallory dropped it into her bag with hardly a glance. They walked and walked.

Alice pointed out augers and cockles and coquinas. She liked teaching Mallory the names of the shells, although sometimes her student was less than attentive.

Because she was looking down and focusing her attention so precisely, Alice lost track of time and of herself. She wouldn't be able to put it into words, except to say she felt removed from the world. Or just at its edge. At the edge of the wild and beautiful world. She felt small, too. But part of something large. She was happy.

Mallory brought her back to the here and now with the questions: "What's this? Is it rare?"

"That is a kitten's paw," Alice told her.

As soon as she heard the name, kitten's paws became Mallory's favorite. "Kitten's paws are the best," she said emphatically. "And they really look like kitten's paws. I'm going to try to collect hundreds of them."

She crouched like a kitten and pounced when she saw one. "Meow," she said.

After that, Alice concentrated on her own collecting. To her, kitten's paws were ordinary. She found two good things—a perfect shark's eye and a tiny bright orange conch no bigger than a fly. They brought her boundless satisfaction.

"Let's turn around and head back," Kate called.

Alice had forgotten about Kate. She'd been lagging behind, giving Alice and Mallory plenty of space. Now Alice wanted to be with Kate, and so after they turned around, they walked together, arm in arm, with Mallory just ahead of them, still consumed with her search for kitten's paws.

The sun was softening. Banks of clouds sat on the western horizon like great cottony hedgerows with deep lilac shadows.

"What do you want for your birthday dinner this year?" asked Kate.

"Same as always," replied Alice. "Hot dogs on the grill and key lime pie and chocolate cake."

"You're the only person I know who gets a pie *and* a cake for her birthday."

Alice giggled and tipped her head to one side.

They unlocked their arms but remained close together, Alice's shoulder brushing against Kate every few strides.

They talked about school and clothes and books. They talked about Alice's friends and about Helen Blair. Alice wanted to ask Kate about Mallory and Ted but was suddenly overcome with a bout of shyness.

A comfortable, uncomplicated silence passed between them. Alice watched the water for dolphins, and then she watched Mallory.

Mallory had wandered away from the surf toward

a clump of pale, tufty grass that crept down to the ocean. Alice saw her stoop low—opposite the direction of the bent-over grass—then spring back up with something in her hands.

"Look what I found!" Mallory screamed. She ran directly to Alice. "Is it a junonia? It's something good, I can tell. Right?" Her eyes were flashing.

It was an old conch, riddled with tiny holes and spotted with tar. It was about nine inches long. To Alice, it looked like the tooth of a dinosaur.

"It's not a junonia," said Alice. "But it's good. It's a nice, big, old conch."

"It's really not a giant junonia?" Mallory asked wistfully.

"No," said Alice.

Mallory's face fell. The glow she'd had about her just seconds earlier had dimmed to nothing.

"I like it," said Kate. "It's so big."

"I'm tired," said Mallory. She mumbled something else and handed the conch to Alice.

Alice lifted the shell to her ear. She narrowed her eyes, then closed them. "You can hear the ocean," said Alice. "I love that." She gave the shell back to Mallory. "Try it. It's nice."

Mallory clamped the opening of the shell over her ear. An odd expression crossed her face. "Mama?" she whispered. "Mama?" She waited a long moment, then put the conch into her bag. With one quick jerk, she pulled Munchkey from the crook of Kate's arm and trudged on.

Alice looked up at Kate, searching her face. Their eyes caught and locked. "I'll tell you later," Kate said quietly.

CHAPTER 8

It was Alice's mother, not Kate, who told Alice about Mallory. They were alone in the living room of Scallop, sitting on the saggy couch. Alice's mother said that Mallory's parents were divorced, and that Mallory's mother had gone to France for a while and no one knew when she'd return.

Suddenly, certain things made sense to Alice. Now Alice understood why Mallory had said that Munchkey's mother had gone to sea in a pot. And she knew why Mallory had called "Mama?" into the conch.

"Can't Mallory talk to her mom on the phone?" Alice asked.

"I don't know all the particulars," said Alice's mother. She continued, her tone milder. "But it seems complicated, and it makes me feel sorry for Mallory."

"Yeah," said Alice absently. She was thinking how annoying Mallory could be. She was also thinking that if the details of her life and Mallory's life were interchanged, she, Alice, would be miserable. "You would never do that," said Alice.

"What, honey?"

"Leave me."

Her mother shook her head. "But I *am* going to leave you temporarily. I need to take a shower before we go to the Wishmeiers'."

Alice leaned into her mother to make her stay. In

response, her mother leaned into Alice. At that very moment, Alice loved her mother so completely she thought they might fuse together and melt away.

Smiling, Alice's mother rose. She crossed the tiny living room toward the tiny bathroom.

"Are Kate and Ted and Mallory coming?" Alice already knew the answer.

"Yes," her mother called. "Mr. Barden, too. Dad's already there. You can go over."

"I'll wait for you," said Alice. She ended up sitting on the floor in the cramped hallway, her back against the closed bathroom door, until her mother was ready to leave.

Mr. Wishmeier greeted Alice and her mother as they approached the Wishmeiers' patio, which was not much bigger than a large quilt. Behind him, Alice's father, Ted, and Mr. Barden were circling a small grill spilling over with fire. Mr. Wishmeier was impeccably dressed in a crisp white shirt, plaid pants, and his straw hat. "Now the party can start," he said.

Alice glanced around quickly, wondering if this was some sort of surprise for her. Prickles of excitement broke out along her neck. "It's not my birthday yet," she said, her voice high and expectant. "It's not till the day after tomorrow." Her eyes widened and she glanced around again, grinning, waiting.

There was no reaction, except a nod from Mr. Wishmeier, and Alice realized that he hadn't been referring to her birthday but had simply been using a figure of speech. There was no surprise.

Alice blushed. She wanted to vanish. Just forget it, she told herself. No one noticed. No one cares.

But her mother noticed. She patted Alice's shoulder and said, cheerfully and calmly, "We've got birthday on the brain."

Mr. Wishmeier smiled. "Well," he said, "the women are all inside."

Alice moved closer to the grill. The fire was hypnotic. It was like a snarl of orange scarves caught in a frantic wind. Mr. Wishmeier checked the flames from all angles. The way he did this—craning his neck left and right, moving forward, then backward—caused his wide-brimmed hat to take on the appearance of a platter he was trying to balance on his head.

Alice was torn—she was drawn to the fire, but she thought her lingering embarrassment might go away faster if she went inside. After a slight hesitation, she followed her mother into the Wishmeiers' kitchen.

Mrs. Wishmeier was trying to get Mallory to smile. She was fixing lettuce for a salad. She tore a long, thin, ripply piece and held it up to her face as if it were a green mustache.

Mallory barely responded. Her lips twitched—that was all.

Mrs. Wishmeier tried harder. She continued to hold the lettuce under her nose, and made funny faces—first, arching one eyebrow, then flaring her nostrils. When neither of those attempts worked, she crossed her eyes.

Alice erupted with pure, joyful laughter. So did her mother, and so did Kate.

Remote as the moon, Mallory sat stiffly on a stool at the kitchen table with Munchkey on her lap. Before her, on the table, was a small mound of kitten's paws. "Can I draw?" she asked, fingering the shells.

Mrs. Wishmeier sighed. "Yes, you *may*," she said pointedly. She tossed the piece of lettuce into the sink and rummaged about the crowded kitchen counter. "Here's a notebook," she told Mallory. "And something in here should work for you." She plopped an old chipped mug down onto the table within Mallory's reach. The mug was filled with pens, pencils, and markers.

It seemed to Alice that Mrs. Wishmeier was losing her patience with Mallory, but she was as sweet as ever to Alice. She asked Alice to arrange crackers on a plate and to put potato chips in a bowl.

Alice's mother and Kate kept busy with Mrs. Wishmeier, finishing the salad and preparing vegetables and fish for the grill.

Everyone asked Mallory if she wanted to help, but Mallory only wanted to draw.

When Alice completed her tasks, she sat on a stool in the corner. She sniffed the backs of her hands. They had the wonderful, warm sunscreen smell. Then she pulled up her right knee and bent over and breathed in deeply. Her knee smelled even better than her hands. Alice hugged herself.

From where she sat, Alice could see that Mallory was tracing around kitten's paws with a black marker in the notebook. Mallory would cover a page—row upon row—then fill another page. "Meow," she'd say softly every few minutes.

Watching this made Alice sad for some reason, so she watched the women instead. How could she ever be as old as Mrs. Wishmeier? she wondered. It seemed impossible. What would she look like when she was her mother's age? It was all as mysterious as anything in the world could be.

Suddenly Mallory shrieked. The sound was piercing, the plaintive cry of a wounded animal. Mallory let herself fall to the floor in a heap. She'd dragged Munchkey down with her. The black marker rolled under the table and several kitten's paws scattered around the room. "It's permanent!" she wailed. "It's permanent!"

Everyone came to her side as if pulled by ropes.

Ted rushed in from the patio. He scooped her up and took her to the couch. He cradled and rocked and hugged her.

Between huge gasps and sobs, Mallory could be heard to say, "I wanted Munchkey to be a kitten"—gasp—"so I gave her whiskers"—sob—"but I hate it"—gasp—"and it's a permanent marker"—sob—"and now Munchkey's ruined." Then came hysterical crying and nose-blowing into Ted's shirt. Mallory shook uncontrollably before settling into Ted like a sleeping baby.

It all seemed so private to Alice, and yet she couldn't keep from staring at them. She felt relieved when Ted carried Mallory and Munchkey away. Alice quietly said good night to them. When they passed by her, she caught a glimpse of Munchkey. The whiskers were jagged dark streaks on the pale blue corduroy.

"We'll be back or we won't," Ted said on the threshold, turning to face them. "Don't wait for us."

As Ted walked off, Mallory lifted her head and gazed over her father's shoulder at Alice. Mallory's hair was mussed—a flurry of yellow. Her eyes were red rimmed and empty. She looked lost.

CHAPTER 9

"The storm has temporarily passed," Mrs. Wishmeier whispered to Alice as everyone sat down to eat. But Alice found herself thinking about Mallory throughout dinner. Ted and Mallory never came back, and Alice wondered what they were doing. Had Ted fixed Munchkey? Did Mallory eat anything? Was she sleeping?

After dinner, Kate left to check on Mallory and Ted, and the rest of the group played cards. Alice's favorite was Crazy Eights.

"I'm going to see how things are with Mallory," Alice's mother said at the end of their third game.

"Can I go with you?" asked Alice.

"No, play without me," her mother replied.

"Well, I need to go to bed anyway," said Mr. Barden. "I'm tired." He grabbed his cane from where he'd hooked it on the back of his chair and pushed himself up slowly and awkwardly.

"I should start cleaning up," said Mrs. Wishmeier.

"I'll help you," said Alice's father.

"I'll walk you home," Mr. Wishmeier said to Mr. Barden.

Alice was feeling deserted.

"Alice," said her father, "why don't you collect the cards, then help in the kitchen."

"*Or,*" said Mr. Wishmeier, "walk Mr. Barden home with me. If it's all right with your parents."

Both Alice's mother and father nodded.

Alice decided to go with Mr. Wishmeier.

"Oh, good," said Mr. Barden, "the quiet one is coming with us."

They walked at a turtle's pace. The night air was cool. Stars littered the black sky like crushed ice. No one spoke most of the way, so Alice listened to the palm fronds rustling overhead and the rhythmic pounding of the waves.

"Good night, good night," Mr. Barden said at his door. "Thank you for the evening. That little blond one sure is a screamer, but she is the prettiest girl I ever saw."

The words stung. Tears welled up in Alice's eyes.

Alice knew that she wasn't the prettiest girl in the world, and who cared anyway? But Mr. Barden was supposed to be *her* friend, not Mallory's. He'd been disloyal and had hurt her feelings, and she thought that by the time you were his age, you'd know better.

She was convinced that Mr. Barden wouldn't have made his remark if she didn't have her speck. She had forgiven him when he'd tried to wipe it away yesterday, but this was different.

Alice raised her hand to her face, near the corner of her mouth, and covered the little brown spot.

The short walk back seemed miles long.

Mr. Wishmeier broke the unbearable silence. "In the areas of charm, wit, grace, and beauty, you have no match," he said.

Kind as it was, Mr. Wishmeier's comment did little to lessen the effect of Mr. Barden's. Alice couldn't even say thank you because she knew that if she opened her mouth to speak, she'd cry.

Alice successfully fought off tears until her family was in their cottage getting ready for bed. She could feel herself weakening.

"What's wrong, sweetie?" her mother asked.

Alice shrugged. If she told her parents about Mr. Barden, she knew what they'd say. She'd heard it too many times before. They'd say how pretty she was and how her speck made her who she was and that it wasn't called a beauty mark for no reason.

"Is it the whole Mallory thing?" asked her father.

Alice nodded. She couldn't tell them what was really bothering her, but she couldn't contain her emotions any longer. She nodded again, then started to cry. She'd been all knotted up, and now, alone with her parents, she felt like a fist unclenching.

"Let's sit down," said Alice's father.

They shuffled over to the couch and huddled together. Alice's father had grabbed a handful of tissues from the kitchen table; he gave it to Alice. She wiped her eyes and cheeks and blew her nose.

"Mallory's having a difficult time," said Alice's

mother. "And I know it can be upsetting to see someone so unhappy."

"Is she okay?" asked Alice.

"I think so. When I checked next door, she was sleeping. She must have been exhausted."

Alice's breathing soon became regular again. She
tried to match her breathing to her parents'.

After a few moments of quiet, Alice's father said,
"Would you like a little bed supper tonight?"

"Yes," whispered Alice.

The three of them sat on Alice's bed and shared
crackers with peanut butter and a glass of milk.

Alice's father said what he always said when they
had bed supper. Alice knew this mini-speech by
heart and sometimes chimed in. "When I was a
boy," he began, "and was upset at bedtime for whatever reason, your grandma always gave me something small and good to eat, in bed, and I always

felt better." He paused. "Do you feel better?"

"I do," said Alice. She was remembering some of her other Florida bed suppers. There was the night she had stepped on a shell and cut her foot when she went out to look at a full moon. And there was the night she was jumping on her bed after the lights had been turned off; she'd jumped right off the bed and hit her head on the corner of the dresser. She'd had a lump the size of a lime and the color of a blueberry.

"Tomorrow," said Alice's mother, "you and Dad and I will go off by ourselves. We'll do something fun— just the three of us."

"Promise?" said Alice.

"Promise," said her mother.

"And then the next day is your birthday," said Alice's father.

Alice flashed a quick smile, then her mouth turned downward. "What about Munchkey?" she asked.

"Munchkey still has whiskers," said Alice's mother. "And Ted and Kate were still trying to figure out what to do. Who knows? But that's not for you to worry about."

It suddenly struck Alice that she and Munchkey shared a trait. They both had something on their faces that didn't belong.

Her parents kissed her and left her alone in the silvery dark. Already, the dresser, the chair in the corner, and the floor lamp were fuzzy shapes, well on the way to dissolving completely. Alice walked her fingers across her bedspread; it was too murky to see the streets of the Chinese village, but she knew they were there.

She slipped her hands under the covers. The bedsheets were gritty with sand. She moved from her back to her stomach, trying to get comfortable. She imagined Junonia making her speck disappear and magically restoring Munchkey's face. She wondered what she and her parents would do tomorrow. She thought glorious birthday thoughts. But always, at the fringes of her mind, were Mr. Barden's words.

Somehow, somehow, she fell asleep.

CHAPTER 10

Alice's parents kept their promise. The next day the three of them ate an early breakfast, then set out in the car for the nearby bay. Kayaking was first on their list of things to do.

As Alice and her parents drove away from the cottage, Alice saw the Wishmeiers out the rear window of the car. They were walking toward the ocean. Helen Blair's cottage was quiet, as if it were sleeping. There was no sign of Kate, Ted, or Mallory. There was no sign of Mr. Barden anywhere, either.

We're alone together, thought Alice, looking at the backs of her parents' heads. She played with the words in her mind, tumbling them around like stones. Together alone. Alone together. The words seemed opposite, but combined, their meaning was different, and it deepened the more she thought about it. Without realizing it, she said the words aloud. "We're alone together."

"Yes, we are," said her mother.

They'd rented two kayaks. Alice and her mother were in one; her father was in the other by himself. Alice asked if she and her mother could lead. And they did.

They hugged the edge of the bay, then turned into the mangrove swamp. Narrow estuaries wound through the mangrove trees. Each year, Alice thought of these passages as streets made of water.

The tide was coming in. Branches reached out like arms, partially blocking the way. And the roots of the mangroves were like spindly legs rising from the brackish water.

They paddled slowly through the leafy corridors, gliding in and out of light and shadow, following a course marked with small, numbered wooden signs. The water was silver and opaque in places, and transparent in others. It was so quiet that the sounds Alice did hear, including her own breathing and the knocking of the paddles against the sides of the kayak, seemed louder than normal.

Alice saw egrets and herons and one anhinga holding its wings out to dry. In the distance, an ibis walking daintily through the water, probing for food, reminded her of Mr. Barden.

After they came to the last trail marker, they paddled out into the bay and then drifted aimlessly in the open water. Being low in the kayak made the water seem so vast and deep, the sky so far and wide. Alice felt like a dust mite compared to all of it. She whispered, "It's so big."

Her mother turned her head partway and nodded.

Alice wanted to ask her: Do you ever feel too small to matter? But she didn't. She would have felt silly. She let her mind roam until they were back at the shore, climbing out of the kayaks.

From the bay, they drove to the lighthouse at the eastern tip of the island. Alice combed the beach for shells but found nothing worth keeping. She did see several kitten's paws, and debated picking them up for Mallory, but decided against it. She could picture Mallory hating kitten's paws now, never wanting to see one again.

Lunch was next. They chose a restaurant close to

the lighthouse, a restaurant Alice had never been to before. After that, they went to one of the public beaches, where Alice ended up with about a dozen good shells, including a lace murex and four tulips in perfect condition.

The day was unfolding exactly the way Alice had hoped it would.

The only thing Alice didn't like that day was their trip to the cemetery. The cemetery was on Captiva Island, across a small causeway from Sanibel. Alice's parents took her to the cemetery every year, and she usually suffered silently through the visits, hunting for lizards or running her hands over the mottled lambs on the headstones. The lambs were smooth—time and weather had worn away most of the details so that they looked more like clouds than lambs.

Alice's parents thought the cemetery was pretty and

peaceful; it was one of their favorite spots. "Bury me here," her father said every year. Alice thought the cemetery was boring.

If no one else was around, Alice's parents let her swing on the big, white-latticed gate at the entrance. She swung for a while, but it felt babyish to her this year.

While she waited for her parents, Alice read the dates and inscriptions on some of the grave markers. She came upon the graves of twins. ALMA AND TALMA CARTER. BORN MAY 31, 1910. DIED JUNE 1, 1910. Both stones read *Our Darling Baby*.

Suddenly Alice was sad and wanted to leave. She'd never paid much attention to what was written on the markers before. She sat on a rock by the gate. She would sit until her parents were ready to go. To live for only one day was one of the most heartbreaking things Alice had ever considered. The sun on her face was making her sleepy, but she was uneasy, too. She couldn't wait to get away.

A few minutes later, her parents were beside her at the gate. "We could go to a couple of shops," said Alice's mother, "or we could go home and lay low."

Alice liked that her mother had referred to the cottage as home. And at that very second, she realized that she missed Kate. And even Mallory. "Home," Alice replied. "Scallop."

"Good choice," said her father. "Scallop it is. I need a nap."

CHAPTER 11

Alice saw Mallory as the car approached the cottage. Mallory was sitting with her back against the palm tree in front of Helen Blair's place, her knees drawn up.

The instant Mallory spotted the car, she stood and ran toward it, smiling.

"You don't have to play with Mallory if you don't want to," said Alice's mother. "I promised. It can be just us all day."

"I know," said Alice. "It's okay." Alice wanted to

know if Munchkey had been restored to her former self. Munchkey was dangling from Mallory's hand, but Alice couldn't make out her face clearly, couldn't tell if the whiskers had been removed.

When Alice got out of the car, Mallory was right there, in a cheerful polka-dot sundress, still smiling. Alice was surprised at how happy Mallory looked, and she returned a smile, an uncertain one.

"I didn't think you'd *ever* get back!" said Mallory. Her hands were behind her. She was blinking rapidly and wiggling her shoulders, nearly bouncing in place. Munchkey was hidden. "Where have you been?" she asked.

"Well," said Alice, "first we went—"

"I have someone to show you," Mallory announced, interrupting Alice before she could finish her sentence. She presented Munchkey. "Ta-da!" said Mallory.

Munchkey had changed since Alice had last seen

her. Her whiskers had been darkened. Two black tri-angles had been drawn on the top of her bald, pale blue corduroy head. Ears. Her nose, which was a small white bead, now had a bold inverted triangle surrounding it, also drawn with black marker. And she had a yellow-and-green plaid tail, safety-pinned to her backside, made from what Alice recognized as one of Kate's cloth headbands. Munchkey looked more like a cat than ever.

"Wow," said Alice.

"Did you see? She has real paws now," said Mallory.

"I *do* see." They were shells. Kitten's paws had been secured with rubber bands to the ends of Munchkey's arms and legs. "I like the necklace, too," said Alice.

"Kate made it. She found a kitten's paw that had a little hole in it. She strung it on a cord."

For Alice, Munchkey had previously called to mind a sad, flimsy, faded blue rag-doll version of a gingerbread cookie, whose only adornments were the white bead nose, two pink beads for eyes, and a red bead for a mouth. She looked better to Alice now, hodgepodgey, but happy.

Kate came out of her cottage, waved a quick hello, and went inside with Alice's parents.

Mallory leaned closer to Alice. "And the best part is, I changed her name." Mallory was speaking in a very important-sounding whisper. "She's not Munchkey anymore. She's Munch*killy*." Mallory smiled again, proudly.

"That's cute," said Alice. She was wondering how the transformation had occurred. How *both* transformations had occurred. Munchkey wasn't the only one who had been transformed. To have seen Mallory weeping and heaving last night, and then to see her now, was like seeing two completely different people. She'd gone from being miserable to being bubbly. It was as if Junonia were real and she had worked a magical spell. "How did it happen?" asked Alice. "I mean, whose idea was it to actually turn Munchkey into a kitten?"

Mallory shrugged. "I don't really remember. My dad or Kate. I think when my dad couldn't make the whiskers go away, he said maybe they were meant to be. Or something like that. He said that some things in life you can't fix to the way they used to be." She kissed Munchkitty. "My dad says it takes a long time to get used to some things that are new, or when things change. But I'm used to Munchkitty already."

"That was fast," said Alice.

"Yeah, I know. But some things take a long time." She paused, then opened her mouth to say something else, but didn't. She looked away and rubbed her forehead with the heel of her hand.

Alice nodded. She figured that Ted must have been talking to Mallory about her mother as well as about Munchkey. For some reason Alice's mind flickered with thoughts of Alma and Talma Carter. Mallory's mother. The Carter twins. There was a lot of sadness in the world. It was there, even if you didn't notice it at first. Like shadows.

"Let's go," said Mallory. "I want to show Munchkitty to your mom and dad."

"Okay," said Alice, and they went inside together.

After introducing Munchkitty to Alice's parents, Mallory helped Alice wash her shells and line them up on the top of the screened porch railing. They arranged them by type.

"Did you find a junonia today?" asked Mallory.

Alice sighed. "No," she said. "But I really want to find one this year." After all, she was going to be ten. Finding a junonia would be the perfect gift. She picked up one of her new tulip shells and turned it in the light. It was covered with bluish gray and brown markings. Its inner surface was lustrous. It was even more smooth than the lambs at the cemetery. It was many things, but it wasn't a junonia.

"I saw about a million kitten's paws while you were gone," said Mallory, "but my dad says I already have enough and can't keep any more."

Just then Alice's mother called her. "Come here, sweetie. It'll only take a second."

"I'll be right back," Alice told Mallory.

In the far corner of the kitchen, Alice's mother quietly asked Alice if she'd rather have dinner alone—just their family—or if she'd mind eating with Kate, Ted, and Mallory. "It's your choice," her mother said. "Mallory seems happy. . . ."

"Would we eat here or go out?"

"Either. You can decide. It's still your day. Your pre-birthday day."

"Can I pick the restaurant?"

"Sure. But I have veto power."

Alice chose the restaurant she thought Mallory would like best.

"We'll have fun," said Alice's mother. And as Alice turned to go back to Mallory, she added, "You're a good kid."

Alice *did* have fun. And Mallory did, too. Alice thought that everyone did, which made her happy.

Before they ate, Ted proposed a toast in honor of Munchkitty, who was firmly positioned on Mallory's lap. And throughout the meal, Alice and Mallory clinked their glasses together from time to time and said, "Meow."

From their table on the deck at the restaurant, Alice

could see the ocean perfectly. And the sunset. The sky and the sea were full of colors—yellow, peach, pink, blue, green, purple. The water was like liquid color, like melted glass swirling around. Several people were taking photographs. Alice thought that it was one of those sights that would look fake in a photograph, it was so amazing. Or else the photograph wouldn't be able to capture the brilliance of the colors; it would make them dull and ordinary.

Alice watched silently for a few moments, then resumed eating.

Her mother reached out and touched Alice's wrist. "Happy almost-birthday," she whispered. Her face was glowing because of the sunset.

"Happy almost-birthday," Alice whispered back.

CHAPTER 12

When Alice woke up on her birthday, she didn't feel different, but she *was* different. She was ten. And, then, because she *knew* that she was different, she felt different. Ten! She could hardly believe it.

She dressed quickly and went into the kitchen. Her parents were there, waiting under a clutch of balloons hanging from the overhead light fixture. Twisted strands of pink crepe paper were strung from the light fixture to the corners of the ceiling—four loose curves. When Alice had gone to bed, the kitchen had simply been the kitchen. Overnight it had become something new and beautiful and bright. And it was all for her.

"Happy birthday!" said her parents. They spoke in unison, but their voices were separate—high and low—and one complemented the other.

Her father studied her face. "Looking for changes," he said.

Alice laughed.

"Impossible," said her mother. "I can't believe you're ten."

"Believe it," said her father. "Just look at her."

Her parents hustled her out of the cottage into the gray light of morning and down to the water.

"Grab my arm," her mother said when they got to the beach, "and close your eyes."

Alice was led a short distance, which seemed a

hundred miles. "Keep them closed," said her father. She took careful baby steps, and then hands gripped her shoulders and turned her around. This is what it must feel like to be blind, she thought.

"Now you can open them," her father told her.

In front of Alice, above the tide line, was a huge, perfectly formed, heart-shaped mound of sand. Clamshells and cockles had been used to make a border around the heart. Inside the border, more shells, smaller ones, had been used to fashion the word *Alice* and the number *10*. The *i* of *Alice* was dotted with four pieces of sea glass—two pale green, one blue (which is rare), and one red (which is the rarest of all).

Alice couldn't speak at first, but when she could, she said, "I love it."

The decorated kitchen. The sand heart. The blue and red sea glass. How did her parents do such things without her knowing anything about them?

The next moments were a warm blur. Her parents hugged and kissed her. The sky was brightening. Strangers walking by stopped to admire the heart. Suddenly the Wishmeiers were there, too.

"Birthday greetings, miss," said Mr. Wishmeier, tipping his hat. He tapped his walking stick against a piece of driftwood for emphasis.

"Happy birthday," said Mrs. Wishmeier.

Alice smiled. "Thank you," she said.

A woman, a teenaged girl, and a little boy approached. The little boy squealed when he saw the heart. He yelled, "Giant heart!" and charged straight at it. Alice was certain that he was going to ruin it, so she edged over to block his way. The woman was fast. She caught up to the boy and swept him up right before he would have crashed into it.

"Sorry," said the woman. She plopped the boy down and pushed him along in a hasty manner.

"Who would've cared anyway," said the teenager. She curled her lip as she passed. "It's just a stupid heart."

Alice glared at her, but it was more an act than real. She was so happy, the girl's comment couldn't spoil her mood.

"We should take a picture before it's too late," said Alice's mother. She pulled her camera from her pocket and took photographs of the heart with and without Alice. Then Mr. Wishmeier took several photographs of the heart with Alice and her parents kneeling beside it.

The Wishmeiers walked on.

Alice's father called after them, "Cake at our place tonight!"

"And pie!" Alice added.

With a delicate touch, Alice plucked the bits of sea glass off the heart before someone else did. They looked like flower petals in her hand. She smoothed the sand with her other hand. In places, the heart was crusty, and already there were some cracks along the edges. Where Alice straightened one of the shells on the border, she caused a tiny avalanche. She wondered how long the heart would last. It was out of the ocean's reach, but there were always dogs, and there were always nasty kids who enjoy wrecking things for fun. If nothing else, over time, the wind would wear it away.

"When did you find the red and blue glass?" asked Alice.

"Yesterday," replied her mother.

"Where?"

"By the lighthouse."

"How did you . . ." Alice's voice trailed off because something had caught her eye; something stirred inside her. Her mouth hung open. A silvery shape had moved in and out of the water. Her concentration sharpened. She held her breath. The shape reappeared, and after a graceful rolling motion, disappeared again. "A dolphin!" Alice cried, pointing.

The dolphin's fin came and went, came and went. The three of them tried to keep up with the dolphin by jogging along the shoreline. They followed it until it changed course and headed for the horizon.

When it was gone from sight, Alice's father said, "A birthday dolphin. What more could you ask?"

On the way back to the cottage, Alice's heart seized. Mr. Barden was coming toward them. Alice hadn't seen him since he'd made his comment about Mallory two nights ago, and she still felt angry about it, and hurt.

Her parents said hello. Alice kept silent. She managed a tight-lipped, lame smile, and looked above Mr. Barden's head.

"A little bird told me it was your birthday," Mr. Barden said.

Alice nodded. She reached down and scratched her ankle.

"Did the little bird also tell you to come for birthday cake tonight?" said Alice's mother.

"Oooh," said Mr. Barden. His old, bony face expanded with a wide smile, a smile that was a sharp contrast to Alice's skimpy one. "Yes, yes," he said, jingling change in his pocket.

"It won't be too late," said Alice's mother. "One of us will come to get you."

Mr. Barden slipped his hand from his pocket and offered a few coins to Alice. "A little something for the birthday girl," he said.

"Thank you," Alice replied in a soft voice. She forced herself to look right at him as she accepted his small kindness. A part of her remained hardened toward him, but she felt much better. And she was glad to have gotten through this first encounter since he'd made his remark. Seeing him again wouldn't be so awkward for her. She was relieved. She pushed the coins into the same pocket in which she'd put the sea glass.

Alice and her parents waved good-bye and continued on.

Alice wiggled her fingers. Next year she wouldn't be able to count how old she was on her fingers. She'd have more years than fingers. For some reason this fact seemed important. She walked slowly, deliberately, as if by doing so everything about her day would last longer.

"This is my best birthday," said Alice. "Already."

Her father laughed. "You always say that."

"Hey! Hey!" called Mallory. She seemed to have come out of nowhere, galloping directly at them, clutching Munchkitty to her chest with one arm. She stopped abruptly and took a deep breath. "A man from the office brought a package to your porch," she said, her eyes darting wildly. Then her eyes focused on Alice, and she added, "It's the size of a shoe box, and it's for you!"

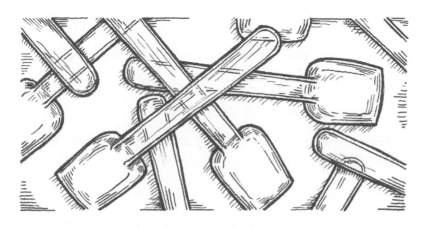

CHAPTER 13

"Why don't you open it?" asked Mallory.

Why don't you say happy birthday? Alice wanted to ask. But she didn't. She lifted her shoulders and kept them raised for the count of ten before dropping them—a nice long careful shrug.

Mallory was leaning over the package and was so close to Alice that Alice could smell Mallory's milky breath.

The package was from Helen Blair. It had come via

overnight mail from New York City. Alice had stared at it, picked it up, shaken it lightly, and brought it into the kitchen and set it down on the table.

"Are you a present waiter?" asked Mallory.

Alice looked at her with a puzzled expression.

"I'm not. I'm a present opener. As soon as possible."

"Oh," said Alice, understanding what Mallory had meant. "I like to wait." There was something wonderful—something potent even—about a present before it's unwrapped. Especially an unexpected one. Anything could be inside.

One of Mallory's curls fell onto the package, one of her fingers traced over the address. "Well?" she said.

Alice sucked on her lower lip, trying to ignore Mallory. She was excited about receiving something in the mail from Helen Blair, and she wanted to hold on to that feeling. She also thought that she might like to open the package without Mallory being there.

She turned her head to the side and looked at her parents over her shoulder.

Her parents and Kate were behind her, drinking coffee and banging around the kitchen making pancakes—measuring flour, cracking eggs, stirring batter. Ted was still sleeping. Kate had pecked Alice on the top of her head and wished her a happy birthday while they were all still outside examining the package.

"Munchkitty wants you to open it," Mallory chirped. Right on cue, Munchkitty's head popped up above the edge of the tabletop. Mallory made Munchkitty take a little bow before she dropped her back onto her lap.

"It's *my* birthday," Alice whispered.

"Oh, yeah," said Mallory. "I forgot to say it. Happy birthday, Alice. I even made you a card yesterday. I'll give it to you later." She blinked several times. "So, are you going to open it?"

Alice puckered her face and cast her glance upward to the ceiling as if it might offer advice. Then, abruptly, she reached forward and let her fingers splay out across the package. She had just begun to pull it closer to her when her father came over and said, "We'll need to move the package to set the table." He was holding a stack of plates. The balloons hanging from the light fixture obscured his face so that he looked like a strange man with numerous ice-cream–colored, eyeless, bald heads. "Did you make up your mind, kiddo? Are you going to open it now, or save it for later?"

"Save it." There. She'd said it.

Mallory slid away from the package and slumped low in her chair, all eagerness drained from her face. She sighed deeply, letting her lips flap loosely as she exhaled. She seemed to be dwindling from disappointment, getting smaller and smaller.

Telling her father had made it official. Alice rose

from the table and scooped up the package. Now she could put the package in her room and enjoy her birthday breakfast, knowing that she could open it later, without Mallory breathing down her neck.

After breakfast, Alice's father used his pocketknife to break the seal on the package from Helen Blair. Mallory and Kate were gone, although Mallory had wanted to stay.

The knife sliced cleanly and easily through the shiny brown tape encircling the box, and the flaps sprang apart with a faint, satisfying sound. "All yours," said Alice's father. He pushed the box across the kitchen table to Alice.

Cushioned between layers of crumpled newspaper, Alice found three small boxes wrapped and tied in orange and purple, and a note. The note was written in a beautiful, slanted cursive hand.

"What does it say?" asked Alice's mother.

Alice read the note aloud.

> *Dear Alice,*
>
> *The snow seems endless here. Yesterday, people were walking and skiing down the middle of Lexington Avenue! And it's cold—everyone has cherries on their cheeks.*
>
> *I miss you all, but the airports are still a mess, and so I've decided to stay put. I hope you've found someone to play Sweet or Sour with.*
>
> *The enclosed birthday gifts are from my trip to Venice this past summer. The little spoons are gelato spoons. I saved them because they seemed too pretty not to keep. The beads were too pretty not to buy. And the euros were in the bottom of my suitcase*

when I returned home. You can use them when you go to Venice one day. And you will. It's heaven. Like being dropped into a jewelry box.

Love to all,

Helen

P.S. If I'm not mistaken, you're ten this year. Ten is a big deal.

"I can't believe she knew you were ten," said Alice's mother.

"I can't believe you can ski down the middle of Lexington Avenue," said Alice's father.

Alice quickly tore into the three small boxes. Even though the note had described the gifts, Alice couldn't wait to see the items, to touch them, to hold them.

There were ten gelato spoons in the first box. The

spoons were just a few inches long. They were transparent colored plastic—two pink, one blue, one green, two purple, one orange, and three yellow. They were smooth and light.

There were ten glass beads in the second box. The beads were multicolored and looked like pieces of hard candy. Alice inspected each one, trying to pick a favorite, but couldn't.

The last box held ten euros. The euros seemed more exotic than American money because each coin was both silver and gold, and was heavy.

"This is so nice of her," Alice's mother said, fingering the beads.

"*So* nice," echoed Alice's father.

Alice nodded vigorously. She started to reread the note. "What does 'cherries on their cheeks' mean?" she asked.

Alice's mother gently patted Alice's face. "Rosy

cheeks—pink cheeks—from the cold air."

"Oh, right," said Alice. She continued to reread the note. She now wanted to know everything about Venice. She knew some about the canals, and she'd seen photographs of a cathedral in one of her father's thick architecture books, but that was the extent of her knowledge. Alice had never been out of the country, and she'd only been in five states: Wisconsin, Illinois, Michigan, Minnesota, and Florida. "Have you ever been to Venice?" she asked her parents.

"No," her father answered, shaking his head.

"Could we go someday?"

"Maybe," said her father.

Her mother sighed. "I've always wanted to see Italy."

When Alice was done looking at her gifts—absorbing them—she put them back into the small boxes. Then she replaced those boxes in the carton in which they'd been shipped. The boxes were settled snugly amid the crumpled newspaper like eggs in a nest.

"Hey, maybe we could use the gelato spoons at my party tonight," said Alice. "For ice cream."

"Sure," said her mother.

"But everyone has to give them back because I want to keep them." Forever, thought Alice. Forever and ever.

CHAPTER 14

On the sun-drenched afternoon of her tenth birthday, while her mother finished making a chocolate cake and a key lime pie, Alice and her father checked the sand heart before setting off on a junonia walk. Alice hadn't told him it was a junonia walk; she'd kept that to herself. He thought they were simply taking a stroll on the beach.

Alice had the red and blue sea glass, one of the gelato spoons, one bead, one euro, and a dime from

Mr. Barden in her pocket for good luck.

If she really listened, Alice could hear the word *junonia* in the sound of the waves. The whispering voice of the ocean coaxed her on, and she wished with all her might that she'd find a junonia, knew that she would if only she concentrated hard enough and walked a little farther, a little bit farther.

With her head bent downward, her eyes swept left right, left right. All at once, she became aware of her father's toenails. They were thick and yellowed like jingle shells. They looked like the toenails of an old man, and she glanced up to make sure her father was still her father.

"Yes?" he said. He raised his eyebrows above his sunglasses.

She smiled at him. "Nothing."

"Did I wish you a happy birthday?" he asked. Now he wiggled his eyebrows.

Alice wrinkled her nose. "A hundred times."

"Just checking."

A sudden rush of warm wind tossed Alice's hair, and a few strands caught in the corner of her mouth. She left them there.

"You look like you're searching for something," said her father. "Something specific."

She told him.

"Well," he said, "I wouldn't get my heart set on finding a junonia. I've never seen one."

"But people do," she said. And it's my birthday, she thought. And I'm ten today, which is extra special.

Alice's father flicked his wrist and checked his watch. "We should turn back," he said.

"Already?"

"I think so."

Alice didn't object, only because she reasoned that a junonia might have washed up behind them. She often found new things on the beach by retracing her steps.

On the way home, Alice grabbed a thin piece of driftwood. She drew a letter J in the cool, wet, hard, dark sand right after a wave had receded, and she drew another one up on the warm, dry, soft, lighter sand away from the surf. She made two wishes. One of the Js would be washed away in minutes; the other would last longer but would be trampled to nothing soon enough by people walking by. She threw the driftwood into the water and made another wish.

"Do you remember your tenth birthday?" she asked her father, without looking up.

"I don't."

"Really?" That seemed impossible. Alice smiled privately. She'd never forget hers. She found another piece of driftwood—a chunky one, like a melon—and heaved it at a wave.

"Nice toss." The voice was low and came from behind them. They turned around. It was Mr. Wishmeier. Alice and her father waited for him to catch up to them. He moved briskly and soundlessly with his walking stick.

"What treasures have you found today?" asked Mr. Wishmeier. "Other than your birthday heart."

Alice extended her open hands for Mr. Wishmeier to see—palms up, palms down, palms up. Empty.

"Apparently," said Alice's father, "we're on a mission. A junonia mission."

At least, Alice noted, he hadn't said a *hopeless* junonia mission. "Have you ever found one?" she asked, squinting up at Mr. Wishmeier.

"I haven't. But my son Allen did once, long ago, when he was about your age."

"See, Dad," said Alice. "I *really* want to find one." This sentence, although not spoken loudly, was brimming with emotion, and was directed at her father, at Mr. Wishmeier, at the clouds, at the sun-shine, at the sand, at the ocean. For a second, while she'd formed the words, the feeling of wanting took up her whole body.

"Just remember to enjoy the hunt," Mr. Wishmeier commented warmly. "That's the important thing," he added, already picking up his pace. When he was a few yards ahead of them, he raised his walking stick as if to say good-bye and good luck.

Alice kept searching.

"Junonia or not—" Alice's father began.

"I know," Alice cut in.

The ocean continued to chant *junonia*, but to no avail. The little cottages, including Scallop, were soon in view. And so was Alice's mother, waiting, waving.

"More birthday, here we come," said Alice's father.

CHAPTER 15

Mallory was all stirred up. She blew into Alice's bedroom like a trumpet blast. She wanted Alice to look at the birthday card she'd made for her and to open the present she'd brought over.

Alice could tell that Mallory would not settle down until she complied.

"The card's a drawing of Munchkitty," Mallory explained. "With a party hat."

"It's really nice," said Alice.

The present was rolled up in yellow tissue paper and tied with ribbon at both ends so that it looked like a party favor, a cracker, the kind Alice always found in her stocking on Christmas morning. Alice sat on the edge of the bed with the present on her lap.

"Open, open," said Mallory, rising up on her tiptoes. She came down heavily on her heels, then plopped onto the bed next to Alice. The mattress was so soft they sank into each other, bumping shoulders. Mallory tried to make Munchkitty sit up on the bed beside her, but the doll collapsed on herself. "She's sleeping," said Mallory, flipping out her hand in a dismissive gesture. "Now, open."

"Okay," said Alice. She moved over a little, away from Mallory, and turned slightly to better face her.

The present. It was a homemade necklace—a kitten's paw on a cord. A match to the one Munchkitty was wearing.

"Thank you," said Alice.

"Put it on," said Mallory. "And see, I've got one, too." She snaked her hand under her shirt and pulled out a necklace of her own. "We're triplets!" She thrust her chin into her chest and peered downward while she talked. "My dad says the holes are called boreholes and that something ate it to make the hole." She lifted her chin and took a deep breath. She watched Alice. "I found the shells after breakfast."

Alice looped the necklace over her head and gently pulled the shell to straighten it.

Mallory calmed down a bit, until she remembered about the box from Helen Blair. When Alice told her she'd opened it, Mallory begged to see the gifts.

Mallory was most interested in the gelato spoons. "The little spoons would be *perfect* for Munchkitty!" said Mallory. "They could be shovels for when she goes to the beach." As she spoke her eyes widened and her voice rose and quickened.

They were lying on the bed, the spoons between them. Mallory picked up the spoons and arranged them into a wheel, handles in the center. Before she placed the single blue spoon down, she'd caressed it as if it were a tiny animal.

It was strange to Alice how the gelato spoons were becoming more and more desirable to both of them with each passing second. Alice surrounded the spoons with her arms, protecting them.

"You have a lot of them," said Mallory. Her eyes were pleading, and they were glittering with determination, too. She was propped up on her elbows, twisting a strand of her hair around her pinkie.

"I have ten," Alice replied. "Because *I'm* ten. No extras," she said quietly as she gathered up the spoons. "I'll put them away, but we can use them later for ice cream."

"You should count them again," said Mallory. Her gaze was fixed on Alice as Alice crossed the room and hastily shoved the spoons into a dresser drawer. "Maybe you have eleven."

Alice felt the beginnings of a growl uncurl deep within her. "Hey," she said, thinking fast, hoping to divert Mallory, "we could make place cards for dinner."

"How many people will there be?" asked Mallory.

Alice calculated in her head. "Six. My family and you and Kate and your dad."

"What about the old people?"

"The Wishmeiers and Mr. Barden? They're coming later for cake and pie. And ice cream."

"They're not coming for hot dogs?"

"No."

"I am," Mallory said proudly. "Maybe they don't like hot dogs, anyway."

"I don't know." Alice stood by the doorway, her arms

folded across her chest, her hands tucked under her armpits. She let her hair fall over her face like a curtain. "Are you going to help me?" she asked, raking her hair behind her ears.

Mallory bobbed on the bed as if she were riding waves. It was clear to Alice that she was considering the idea. With her hair bouncing, she sprang from the bed, causing it to shift and the legs of its metal frame to scrape against the floor. "But we have to do a place card for Munchkitty, too," she said in a funny cadence, almost like a song or a nursery rhyme.

"Of course," said Alice.

Mallory forgot about the spoons, and she and Alice busied themselves making place cards—cutting paper, lettering names, and drawing a picture of a shell on each one.

Before Alice knew it, the place cards were in their

proper spots, the hot dogs were ready, and she was eating her birthday dinner. The hot dogs were perfect. The potato chips were perfect. Even the carrot sticks were perfect; they were sweeter than ever, and crunchy, and the most pure orange color imaginable. Can food somehow know it's your birthday and change to become more delicious? Underneath it all lay the faded red-and-white–checked tablecloth that Alice's mother had found in the back of the cupboard. It was perfect, too.

The balloons and the crepe paper swayed gently overhead while they ate. Alice's mother had turned on the air conditioner because of all the baking she'd done. It clicked and hummed like a chorus of insects. The pie was in the refrigerator. The cake would be a surprise; it was hidden somewhere. There was a little pile of presents in the corner.

The room was small to start, and with Alice and

her parents and Mallory and Kate and Ted and Munchkitty and the balloons and the crepe paper filling it up, the room was even smaller. Everything was close, and yet Alice felt a clear space all around her, like a bubble. A perfect birthday bubble.

CHAPTER 16

After dinner, but before the Wishmeiers and Mr. Barden came for cake, Alice opened her presents. Kate gave Alice a fluorescent tie-dyed T-shirt, a cloth headband with peace signs printed on it, and a fancy pen. From her parents, Alice got books, a bulky cable-knit sweater she'd seen in a catalog and asked for, a small oval mirror framed in gold that her mother had found in an antique store, and a bracelet with a silver sand-dollar charm attached. There was one last present from her parents. Alice decided to save it until later. She wanted one present to open before bed.

Alice had put on the headband and the bracelet right away. Every few seconds she glanced at the bracelet, admiring it. It wasn't too heavy, but heavy enough that Alice knew it wasn't from a drugstore or something she'd buy with her own money, unless she'd been saving for it a long time.

As soon as the Wishmeiers and Mr. Barden arrived, the room was darkened, the cake was presented, and everyone sang.

"Happy birthday to you . . ."

The cake was a round layer cake. The sides were frosted in the palest pink and dotted with little chocolate florets. The top was white, with a junonia outlined and decorated in chocolate icing. Ten white candles were evenly spaced, forming a ring of fire around the junonia.

The candle flames flickered and cast a yellow glow on each smiling, singing face. Alice stared at the flames until she saw through them, and then her eyes seemed only to register the candlelight and the bursts of light from the camera flash. Nothing else in the world existed.

"Happy birthday, dear Alice, happy birthday to you!"

With one big breath, Alice blew out all ten candles. She felt like a deflated balloon, but she'd done it. And she hoped that her wish to find a real junonia would come true. And she sensed once again that she was a different person than the one she'd been yesterday.

Gasping, she marveled at her cake; it was almost too beautiful to eat.

"Can you tell what it's supposed to be?" asked her mother.

"Of course," whispered Alice.

"I can't," said Mallory. "What is it?"

"A junonia," said Alice.

"I thought it was an alien or something," said Mallory. "A monster with lots of spots." She cocked her eyebrows and wagged her head from side to side. "Oh, now I see it!"

The lights were back on. Alice's mother was cutting the cake, Alice's father was cutting the pie, and Kate was taking orders for ice cream. Mallory made sure that she had the blue gelato spoon at her place, and she'd gotten the orange one for Munchkitty.

"Well," said Mr. Wishmeier, "no matter what happens, you can truthfully say you got a junonia on your tenth birthday."

Alice smiled at him.

"Ten," said Mr. Barden. "I'm so old, if you lined up all my birthday cakes they'd reach from here to the middle of the Gulf of Mexico."

Alice's father turned on the coffeemaker and poured

milk for Alice and Mallory. Everyone was cheerful and talkative. There wasn't room for all of them at the table, so Alice's father and Ted stood to the side, leaning against the kitchen counter.

Alice swelled with happiness. She settled back contentedly in her chair. All of the pieces of this particular day had come together to make her birthday. As an attempt to prolong that feeling, Alice took small, dainty cat bites of her cake. When she dipped forward and used her pink gelato spoon to taste the ice cream, she thought of Helen Blair.

While the adults complimented Alice's mother's baking, Alice was wondering how many people in the world shared her birthday. How many people were celebrating at this very moment.

Barely audibly at first, and quickly growing louder, Mallory started humming "Happy Birthday." Munchkitty was her chosen audience. Taking a gelato

spoon in each hand, Mallory imitated a conductor—
her version, with two batons.

Ted's cell phone rang, and Alice jumped. It almost
sounded like an accompaniment to Mallory's humming. The room went quiet.

"Hello?" said Ted, turning away from everyone.
"Tricia?"

"Mama?" said Mallory. "Mama?" Her anxious into-
nation made the word feel terribly huge.

"Be quiet, Mallory. I can't hear," Ted said harshly.

"Is it Mama?"

Ted nodded as he walked out of the room toward the
front door.

Mrs. Wishmeier brought her hand up to her mouth
in a gesture of sincere concern. "Isn't she in France?"
she asked, directing her question vaguely at Kate.
"And isn't it the middle of the night there?"

Mallory's face was a blur as she shot up to follow her

father. She accidentally bumped the table. The sudden movement knocked over her glass of milk, and Alice's, too. The milk from one glass splashed across the table, the other spilled all over Mr. Barden, pooling on his pants. The glasses rolled but remained on the table.

There was a silence, and then Mr. Barden's voice seared it. "Oh, bloody hell!" he rasped. He fixed his eyes on his lap and clutched himself with nervous hands. "It looks like I wet my pants." He kept moistening his lips and blinking. "I hate birthdays," he muttered.

Watching and listening to Mr. Barden hollowed Alice's insides. He was like a spidery old sea creature washed up on the beach. Alice didn't dare risk a movement, except to choke down the bite of cake already in her mouth.

Time turned strangely elastic—seeming to flow in

slow motion, but flowing faster than usual, too. How could that be?

Kate plucked Munchkitty from the floor and followed Mallory, who had disappeared out the front door after her father.

The Wishmeiers and Alice's father were helping Mr. Barden. They mopped him up with napkins and moved the dripping edge of the tablecloth up onto the table, away from him. With paper towels, Alice's father wiped the floor. "You'll be fine," Mrs. Wishmeier assured him.

"I *am* fine," said Mr. Barden, his voice thin and brittle. "I just want to go home." His breath whistled in his nostrils.

In a wordless shuffle, Alice's father and Mr. Wishmeier ushered Mr. Barden out of the cottage. At the doorway, Alice's father turned and winked at Alice. He raised his index finger and mouthed, "Be right back."

Without one bit of fuss, Alice's mother cleared the table. She efficiently gathered the four corners of the tablecloth, bunched up the tablecloth, and put it in the sink. Her face was as serene and peaceful as ever. She approached Alice and placed her hands on her daughter's tight shoulders, squeezing gently and rhythmically, a mini massage. "No big deal," she said. She gave Alice an encouraging kiss on her head. "It's hard to know what to clean up or how long to wait. I'll put the ice cream in the freezer, then let's enjoy ourselves, the three of us."

"Good thing the coffee hadn't been served," said Mrs. Wishmeier. "Then we *really* would have had a scene." She was wiping off the table with a damp dishcloth in grand, sweeping arcs. Then she and Alice's mother glided smoothly around the table, neatly replacing the cake platter, the pie plate, Alice's half-eaten piece of cake, a new glass of milk for Alice.

"Birthdays don't happen every day," said Mrs. Wishmeier. "I'm going to have just a sliver more of cake. And I could use a cup of coffee." She helped herself.

The room looked nearly the same as it had before the guests had arrived—except for the missing table-cloth—and yet Alice didn't feel the same at all. She was sad and angry—a combination that was much worse than one or the other. More frustrating. She burned for things to be different. If her birthday were a drawing, the defining outlines that had been laid down throughout the day and the pleasing shapes that had formed would be breaking up, disintegrating, would be partially erased.

The room was engulfed in uncertainty. Who was coming back to finish the party? When would they return? Would anyone be in a happy mood?

Some things, however, were clear. Alice would have

to wait a whole year for another birthday. She'd never turn ten again.

"This is still a very happy birthday," her mother told her. "I'm sure Dad and Mr. Wishmeier will have more to eat when they get back. We can play cards or a board game. Something." She paused. "Don't be mad at Mr. Barden. And don't worry about him, either." She paused again. "Accidents happen. Mallory didn't mean it. And hopefully she's having a nice talk with her mother, right now." Her voice was unconvincing to Alice. She spoke softly. "Remember, no big deal."

For her mother's sake, Alice tried not to care or to feel sorry for herself, but it was impossible.

Ten *was* a big deal. Even Helen Blair had said so in her letter. With a sinking feeling, Alice realized that her birthday had become a big deal, but in a bad way. And she blamed it all on Mallory.

CHAPTER 17

"Mr. Barden'll be fine," said Alice's father, looking right at Alice, holding her gaze. "He's embarrassed more than anything."

"He repeatedly said how sorry he was," added Mr. Wishmeier.

"Any word from Kate?" asked Alice's father.

"No," replied Alice's mother.

"Well, I'm ready for more party," said Alice's father. He heartily clapped his hands once before sitting down at the table. He raised his plate toward Mrs. Wishmeier, who was closest to the pie. "More pie, please."

The party resumed, but it was subdued, or at least Alice was, although having her father and Mr. Wishmeier back had brought a measure of hopefulness into the night again.

She was letting her ice cream turn to soup, stirring and stirring with the pink gelato spoon. Only when the ice cream was melted did she eat it. With each spoonful she felt less disappointed, as though there were some correlation between her mood and the ice cream.

"This might make you feel better," said Mr. Wishmeier. He cleared his throat noisily.

"I sense a story coming," said Mrs. Wishmeier. "And I think I know which one." She drummed her fingers on the tabletop and groaned a comical little groan. Alice could tell she was joking.

Mr. Wishmeier cleared his throat again. "I decided to bake a cake all by myself, my first ever, for Judy's—Mrs. Wishmeier's—first birthday after we got married."

Mrs. Wishmeier chuckled. "Oh, dear."

"The cake was nothing fancy, but still, I'd made it from scratch. Chocolate cake. White frosting. Coconut flakes sprinkled on top. A single candle smack in the middle.

"As I carried the cake, ever so proudly, from the kitchen to the dining room, I stepped on our cat. The cat shrieked to high heaven, I tripped, and the cake ended up on the floor."

Alice had been staring at Mr. Wishmeier with held breath, openmouthed.

He finished, "It was one grand mess."

"An understatement," said Mrs. Wishmeier. "We scraped the cake off the floor and tried to salvage it, tried to piece it together. It was a lopsided, crumbly thing, but all in all it was a very nice birthday."

Alice didn't think she liked the Wishmeiers' story. It made her feel sorry for both of them—Mr. Wishmeier for ruining the cake after all of his hard work, and Mrs. Wishmeier for not having the birthday she probably had hoped for. Through all the laughter, Alice asked, "But how did you feel when it happened?"

It was Mrs. Wishmeier who answered. "You know," she said simply, "I don't really recall the feeling. It was so long ago." A big, crooked smile creased her face, attracting Alice's attention to her cheeks, which were as rutted as walnut shells. "But it is one birthday cake I'll never forget. One of the few I remember."

Alice was glad that the Wishmeiers stayed to play cards. First they all played Go Fish, and then the adults taught Alice how to play Hearts. When it was Mr. Wishmeier's turn to deal, Alice's eyes were cemented to his sun-coarsened hands. He could shuffle expertly. He'd form a bridge with the cards, and the cards would snap into place perfectly, like soldiers. To Alice's astonishment, he could cut the deck with one hand. And when he dealt, he'd flick the cards around the table, as though they were being spat out of a machine set at its highest speed.

Alice was just starting to understand Hearts, to grasp the strategy of the game, when Kate walked in and stood on the threshold with her arms extended and both of her hands on the door frame.

"This just isn't working," said Kate. Her voice was tired and exasperated. "This isn't really working for anybody. I think we'll all feel better if we leave. This wasn't a good idea."

"You're going *now*?" asked Alice's mother.

Kate looked around the room sheepishly, nodding.

Alice's father rose and turned off the air conditioner.

Alice thought he did this because what was happening was important. With the door open and the air conditioner off, Alice could hear various sounds, including the rumble of Ted's voice, the car trunk slamming, footsteps on the crushed shells, and the whimpers and wails of Mallory.

"I want to live in France," Alice heard Mallory say. And "I hate living in Florida."

Kate straightened and smoothed her shirt, as if she were stalling the departure.

"Is everything all right in France?" asked Alice's mother.

"Yes," said Kate. "Nothing's changed. Talking to her mother just upset Mallory more. Ted thinks Mallory will be happier if we drive back now. Get her home."

"I forget," said Alice's father. "How long a drive is it?"

"A few hours," said Kate. "The traffic will be light at this time of night."

There were offers of cake and pie and other snacks for the road, all declined by Kate.

"Next year," said Kate. "Next year will be better." She came forward for hugs. "Maybe I'll be alone."

Enfolded within Kate's tight clasp, Alice felt as if she had only a dim understanding of adult life. "Bye, Aunt Kate," she whispered into Kate's shirt. "I love your presents," she added, nuzzling the inside of Kate's arm so that her new headband rubbed against Kate. It was a way of saying "I especially love the headband" without using words.

They all followed Kate outside.

Mallory was already buckled into the backseat of the car, slumped against the door. A wedge of yellow from the light attached to the cottage roof fell right across her. It seemed to Alice as if Mallory's face had shut down. She looked hopeless, homeless. As Alice forced her lips into a grim smile and slowly waggled her fingers in a halfhearted attempt at a wave, she thought, Mallory's the messiest mess of a kid I've ever seen.

Something selfish and something peevish gained strength in Alice as she watched Mallory. But then Mallory tried to look covertly at Alice, and Alice—her shoulders set high—saw it, and Mallory's eyes stayed on her. A change occurred in Alice. The selfishness and the peevishness wavered and lifted. Her shoulders softened.

Alice could tell that Mallory was fumbling around, struggling with the knobs on the door. Seconds later, the window rolled down and Mallory reached out through the charged air and lightly touched Alice's arm. Mallory quickly pulled her hand back and wiped her runny nose. She spoke; her voice was tremulous, but by the time she'd finished, it was strangely serene. "When I was littler and my nose was dripping, I'd say my nose was crying. Mama told me that." Then she rolled up the window and tucked herself into the mottled shadows, using Munchkitty as a pillow.

The rest happened as if in a dream. The car stuttered ahead. It stopped a short distance away, idling, while Ted ran in and out of the office. Then, with a jolt, the car sped into the heavy darkness as if something awful were chasing them.

After saying good night to the Wishmeiers, Alice found herself back inside the cottage by the kitchen sink, flanked by her parents. She was glad that her parents weren't discussing Mallory, Kate, and Ted. She figured they'd do that privately once she was in bed. Alice pressed her finger onto some crumbs on the cake platter and brought her finger to her mouth.

"Do you need a bed supper tonight, Pudding?" asked her father.

"No," said Alice. "Just this." Again she pressed her finger onto some cake crumbs.

"Do you need one last birthday gift?" asked her mother.

"Ah!" Alice said with a quick intake of air. "I forgot."

"I'll get it," said her father.

Alice tore into the gift, standing up. There was an envelope with her name written on it inside a cardboard box. She opened the envelope. It took her a minute to understand the enclosed letter. She twisted her neck and looked up at her parents. "So this means that a sea turtle is being adopted for me?"

"That's right," said her mother.

"You can even choose a name for it," said her father.

"I love it," said Alice. All of a sudden she felt drained to emptiness. Her legs wobbled. She sighed.

"We'll clean up in the morning," said Alice's mother, steering Alice toward her bedroom.

Alice took one last look at the balloons and the remains of the cake and the crumpled wrapping paper and the little pile of dirty gelato spoons beside the stacks of dishes needing washing. Her birthday was over.

In bed, the events of the day fluttered about her mind like the butterflies on her bedspread. Her imagined birthday, the perfect one she'd wished for, had stayed just out of reach. She'd experienced true happiness and its abrupt reversal. And then things had taken a turn for the better and ended up happy again. What a day!

She was too tired to say good night. "I'm ten. . . ." she whispered, her voice slow and sleepy. The dark room shrank around her, swallowing her up till morning.

CHAPTER 18

Alice had been dreaming as she woke up. In the dream she was stretched out on the beach in her bathing suit, and Mallory was bending over her, drawing spots on Alice's arms, legs, and face with a brown marker. "What are you doing?" Alice had asked calmly. To which Mallory had replied, "I'm making you into a junonia."

While Alice lay in bed, the dream retreated from her memory, splintered and faded to nothing more than a strange aftertaste. Then the thing she was most aware of was sound. Rain rattled on the roof. It was pouring. She didn't feel so bad about it. In fact, the weather was perfect, Alice decided. She'd stay inside and really look at her birthday gifts. Sort them, rank them. She hoped the sea was rough, so that later, when the weather cleared, there might be great things to find—maybe even a junonia. She smiled at the ceiling, then she emerged from the covers as if from a shell and padded to the kitchen.

"Morning," said Alice.

"Morning, sleepyhead," said her mother. She was leaning forward over the sink, up to her elbows in suds.

"Where's Dad?"

"He drove to the store to get the newspaper. He peeked in at you to see if you wanted to go with him. He whispered to you, too, and said it seemed that your eyes were sewn shut. Dead to the world."

Alice yawned. "I'm not hungry yet," she said, "but

can I have cake for breakfast when I'm ready?"

Her mother nodded.

"I'll help you with the dishes," Alice offered.

"I'm almost done," said her mother. "You can dry." She bent toward Alice, keeping her hands in the sink.

Alice took the towel that was slung over her mother's shoulder. It was as though her thoughts were braided together with her mother's, because Alice remembered the gelato spoons just as her mother said, "I washed your little spoons from Helen Blair. They're in the dish drainer with the silverware."

Her mother hummed, and Alice sorted through the silverware, separating the gelato spoons and arranging them in a neat row on the counter. Alice couldn't believe it. She rifled through the silverware again and combed through the plates and cups in the wire mesh drainer. She counted the gelato spoons once more and made sure none were stuck together. Her face reddened.

A sharp, gruntlike exhalation escaped her lips.

Her mother stopped humming. "What?" she asked absently.

"She took one of my spoons."

"What?"

"Mallory stole one of my spoons. The blue one. The one she used last night. There was only one blue one, and it's gone."

"Are you sure? It must be here somewhere."

Again Alice pawed through the drainer. Her mother emptied the water from the sink and sifted through the suds. Nothing.

"Let me look here," said her mother. Alice waited impatiently, rocking on her heels, while her mother unballed the crumpled tablecloth. Her mother shook her head. "Sorry," she said.

They checked every logical place, including the floor around the table and the porch. Then Alice threw on her bathing suit and ran out into the chilly rain to search the area where Ted's car had been parked.

When her father returned minutes later, Alice was back inside, soaked, shivering, wrapped in a towel. The disturbance she'd felt inside her had bubbled into full-blown anger.

"She's a thief!" said Alice.

"Who's a thief?" asked her father.

Alice explained the situation.

"You still have nine of them," said her father.

"But I had *ten*. And just because I have nine doesn't make what she did right."

"If she *did* take it," said Alice's mother, "I agree it's wrong. But try to put yourself in her place. And maybe, maybe, she thought it was okay to keep it. That no one would care. That we'd just throw them away."

"*No*," Alice exclaimed. "No. She knew. She knew they were a present."

Her father said, "If one little spoon makes her happy . . ."

Her mother said, "She's such a sad little girl."

The silence that descended upon them was heavy. Alice took the nine gelato spoons and went to her room. She looked at her gifts, but her anger clouded her vision and clotted her thoughts.

When the rain stopped, she hid the kitten's paw necklace from Mallory in her fist and asked her parents' permission to run down to the ocean.

"I'll come right back," Alice told them. "Please. I just want to see if there might be good shells."

Her parents exchanged a glance.

"I'm ten," said Alice.

"Seeing as you're ten," said Alice's father, "how can we say no?"

"Come right back," said her mother. "And you still need to eat breakfast."

The drenching rain had yielded to steamy, rising temperatures. The air rippled. Waves of heat undulated all around as Alice ran to the ocean. The water was flat, like a sheet of glass.

Alice advanced until the water was lapping at her ankles. She threw the necklace. It didn't go far, but far enough. The necklace sank, disappearing beneath the smooth surface without a trace.

When she turned around to go back to the cottage, her face must have revealed the depth and nature of her feelings, because Mr. Wishmeier, who had appeared out of nowhere, surprising her, looked at her sympathetically and, with a hopeful note in his voice, said, "It gets better."

Alice didn't know what to say. Silently she fled. She didn't slow down until the door of the cottage had slapped shut behind her.

≈

For the rest of the day Alice thought about what Mr. Wishmeier had said. What gets better? she wondered. The weather? It had already stopped raining when she'd seen him. The day, in general? Life?

It—whatever it was—did get better, and it didn't. The day was mixed up. Alice had a nice time with her parents—shelling, reading lazily at the beach, splashing in the ocean. But Mallory's ghostly presence hung around like mist. Alice ripped up and threw away the birthday card Mallory had made, but the phantom was not to be rid of so easily. All at once, when she was scrutinizing her birthday presents, the missing blue gelato spoon was the one she liked best, and she longed for it.

Alice didn't find a junonia that day, and she decided that it was a silly waste of time to think about a god named Junonia. Obviously she, Junonia, didn't exist. She hadn't saved Alice's party from being spoiled, and she hadn't stopped Mallory from becoming a thief. However, Alice came up with the idea of officially calling her adopted sea turtle Junonia. And that seemed exactly right.

Another one of the things that did not get better was the sand heart on the beach. It had taken a beating from the rain. "It's worse for wear, but it's still here," said Alice's father.

"But it's not the same," Alice replied sadly. And even though she knew it was ridiculous, Alice felt that this, too, was somehow Mallory's fault.

CHAPTER 19

The next day was so foggy it seemed as if everything would always look milky and be obscured. But on the day following the fog, the sky was so clear, so blue, it was as though every cloud had been driven from the world for all time. Thoughts of Mallory were like that—they'd come and go.

Since she'd thrown the necklace from Mallory into the ocean, Alice had gotten into the routine of running down to the water's edge, alone, with her parents' permission, several times a day. She'd go when she woke up in the morning, before breakfast. She'd go right before dinner. And she'd go between those times. Down and back, quick as could be.

Often Mr. Barden would be outside his cottage, sitting in his chair. No words had been spoken between Alice and Mr. Barden about the party. He seemed older than ever to her now, unpredictable. Sometimes Mr. Wishmeier would be with Mr. Barden. They'd nod and wave, and Mr. Wishmeier would always hoist his walking stick in greeting.

Alice had not been allowed to go to the beach alone in all the years she'd come to Florida, unless she was within her parents' sights. This new independence was exhilarating to her. She was not an adventurous person. She'd only slept over at one person's house— her best friend Libby's. And she'd only done so three or four times. Once, when she was six, she'd gotten lost in a grocery store, and the feeling of hopelessness that had flooded her whole being was still fairly raw if she thought about it deeply enough. But *this* kind of being alone was different, and safe, and made her feel free.

Alice was starting to experience the familiar sensation she always did toward the end of a trip—the sad, empty, lonely feeling that sat in her stomach like a block of ice. Each time she'd run to the ocean, she'd wonder how many more times she'd do this before she went home to Wisconsin. One of them would have to be the last time.

She also wondered where the necklace was. She thought it would be incredible if someone invented special glasses that allowed one to see beneath the water's surface. Wouldn't it be amazing to see exactly where the necklace had ended up, to see the things people had lost, the shipwrecks, all the shells, and all the creatures that moved and lived under the water? It was like trying to envision all the important things—hundreds of them—that happen inside your body when all you can see is the outside of your skin.

It was on the afternoon of the clear, blue day that something extraordinary happened. Alice had taken a straight, deliberate course to the ocean. She waved in a businesslike fashion to Mr. Barden, who was planted in his chair. She waved to Mr. Wishmeier, too. He was up the beach, not far from the spot where Alice typically turned around. She reached the water. Sun glinted like silver stitches fastening the sea to the sky. She turned to run back to the cottage, and froze.

A junonia. It was up near the tideline, off to the side, close to where Mr. Wishmeier stood. Alice's vision narrowed until all she saw was the shell. A great shiver ran down her back. As she rushed toward it, she felt a sense of levitating from the beach.

"No." She heard the word, but it seemed far away, background noise. "No. Stop."

She stooped and reached for the shell. And it was beautiful. The curve of it. The way it wound into a spiral. The brown markings. The impressive size— almost as big as her fist.

Her fingers touched it, and so did the tip of Mr. Wishmeier's walking stick.

It was a heart-sinking moment. Confused, Alice peered up at Mr. Wishmeier. At first he just looked at her without speaking. He took off his hat. The sunlight behind him darkened his face and shone through his thin ears, turning them red. "I'm sorry," he finally said in a mild voice.

Alice didn't understand what was happening. But the happiness she'd felt was as thin as an eggshell, and as easily broken. Was Mr. Wishmeier trying to say that the junonia was his, that he'd seen it first?

She stood up and shifted her weight from one leg to the other.

Mr. Wishmeier's eyes probed Alice's until she had to look away. He said, "Take it, it's yours. It's for you." He paused. "I knew right away it was a mistake, the wrong thing to do. And I'm sorry, so sorry.

"I've watched you coming and going the last couple of days. And I know you've had some disappointments lately. I also knew how badly you wanted a junonia, so I thought that finding a real one would cheer you up."

He regarded her with an expression she couldn't describe. "I bought it at the shell shop," he admitted. "I should have known better. I feel punished just looking at you."

Alice finally understood, and the weight of understanding made her cry. She tried to disguise her tears by coughing. She licked her lips.

Mr. Wishmeier dropped his hat onto the sand and

laid his walking stick beside it. He picked up the junonia and placed it in Alice's hand, pressing her fingers around it with his fingers. "Let's go tell your parents," he said.

While her parents and Mr. Wishmeier talked on the porch, Alice went to her room. After a few moments filled with hushed voices, she heard the rise and fall of regular conversation, and laughter. She didn't want to be mad at Mr. Wishmeier. She didn't think she was. She had a junonia, a real junonia, even though she hadn't gotten it the way she'd always imagined getting one.

She moved the shell around her bedspread, treating it almost as a puzzle piece, seeing how it blended in here, trying to make it fit the pattern there. The junonia looked like an unopened flower or something ancient from China or Egypt or another faraway place.

Alice wondered what made something rare. The alphabet cone she'd found last year was just as pretty as the junonia, if you really considered it. And so was a tulip shell.

She sat up on the bed so she could see herself in the mirror on the wall. Here I am, she thought, Alice Rice, holding a junonia. She ran the shell up and down her cheek. The junonia was so smooth. She slid it along her chin. It struck her, with the suddenness of a sneeze, that the speck near her mouth looked very much like the markings on the junonia.

Cradling the junonia against her chest, she hopped from the bed and moved so close to the mirror her breath fogged it. She turned the shell. It was astonishing how similar some of the smaller spots on the junonia were to her speck. Same size, same color, same shape. She wouldn't have been able to put it into words, but somehow this discovery made her happy.

She smiled at herself, then huffed and puffed at her image so that it disappeared behind a bleary cloud.

Alice joined the adults on the porch. She brought the junonia with her. Mr. Wishmeier told Alice funny anecdotes about his pet cats back home and about the dog he'd had growing up. Then he told her that when he was a boy, his father let him put maple syrup in his milk on special occasions. His stories seemed to be random, just filling space, but then, in a halting manner, he got around to what Alice guessed he really wanted to say. "I couldn't go through with it, because if you'd found out . . ." He sighed. "I didn't want you to feel tricked. I didn't want you to think I tricked you."

"It's okay," said Alice.

Mr. Wishmeier nodded. His face loosened. He appeared to be relieved.

"Let me see it again," said Alice's father.

Alice passed the junonia to him.

He whistled. "It's a beaut," he said, lifting it slightly for all to see.

"It is," said Alice's mother. "It really is."

Alice matched her mother's tone perfectly. "It really is," she repeated.

CHAPTER 20

On the evening before their departure, Alice and her parents started packing their bags. They wouldn't be leaving until around noon the next day, but Alice's parents wanted to get as much done as possible so they wouldn't be rushed in the morning.

Alice put most of her birthday gifts in her lavender backpack so that they would be with her on the airplane. When she placed the nine gelato spoons into the backpack, she felt a burst of anger directed at Mallory. It seemed that an invisible thread bound them together, and always would.

Alice practiced wrapping the junonia in a T-shirt and wedging it carefully and securely among the other things at the top of the backpack. Then she unwrapped it, because she knew she would be looking at it many times before tomorrow. Alice's mother had taken care of the rest of the shells and the sea urchin from Mr. Wishmeier. They were in a box, safe, labeled, ready to be checked when they got to the airport.

Alice's mother decided to do some laundry. Next to the office, in an open-sided shelter with a thatched roof, there was a washer and a dryer for the guests' use. Both machines were coin operated; they were rusty and noisy, too. "I want to wash one load of the smelliest things," she said, sorting through a heap of dirty clothes in the small hallway off the kitchen.

"Who's got quarters?" she asked. "I think the washer and dryer only take quarters."

"I don't have any," said Alice. "Just dimes and pennies. And dollars." She knew this because she'd counted her money after she'd organized her backpack.

"I have some change," said Alice's father. He reached into his pocket and pulled out a handful of coins. "Here," he said, "let's see what we've got." He dumped the coins onto the kitchen table, very near the edge. A few of the coins fell onto the floor.

"There's a quarter," said Alice. She watched it roll across the floor and disappear under the tall cupboard. "I'll get it."

"I'll get these," said Alice's father. He followed two of the coins as they wheeled around and hit the baseboard near the sink. "One quarter and one nickel," he said, bending down and snatching them.

Alice flopped onto the floor and reached blindly into

the shadows beneath the cupboard. She felt around, sweeping her hand back and forth. "I know it's here," she said. "I saw it go under." She squinted into the darkness but couldn't make anything out. Then she held her breath and tried to flatten herself so that she could extend her arm as far as possible. She made one last giant sweep with her hand. Out from under the cupboard, among swirls of dust, slid the quarter, a piece of dried macaroni, and—the blue gelato spoon.

Alice's eyes widened. It couldn't be. But it was.

A wonderful-horrible feeling crept up her neck. She was glad to have her spoon back, but regretful of all the terrible thoughts she'd had about Mallory. She turned red in the face and had the peculiar sensation that the whole world was watching. She picked up the spoon and the quarter and the macaroni and got up off the floor.

"Hey, isn't that your spoon?" asked Alice's father.

"It is," Alice murmured.

"It must have fallen during the commotion with the spilled milk," said her mother. "I can't believe it."

"I can't either," Alice said in a hollow tone. She slipped the quarter into her mother's hand. "I was so mad at Mallory because I thought she stole it."

"But now you can be happy because you know she *didn't*," said her father.

"And she never knew you were mad at her, anyway," said her mother.

"I guess."

Alice fingered the spoon, thinking. The perceptions that she had trusted had already been replaced. She wished that she hadn't thrown the necklace into the ocean. She crossed the kitchen and tossed the macaroni into the wastebasket. "I think I'll send her one of the spoons when we get home," she said quietly.

"That would be very nice," said her mother.

"You're a good kid," said her father. "Did we ever tell you that?"

Alice nodded and flashed him a jack-o'-lantern grin.

Her father narrowed his eyes playfully. "Now don't get a big head."

Alice's mother was counting quarters at the table. "I think we've got enough," she said. "Who wants to help me do laundry?"

Alice went to bed early, but it was always difficult for her to sleep well on the night before a trip—coming or going. Absently she worked her finger through a threadbare spot on the bedspread, creating a small hole. She was thinking about Mallory and the spoon. She not only would send a spoon to Mallory, she decided she'd send one for Munchkitty, too. And she'd send the blue and the orange spoons, because they were the ones Mallory had chosen the night of the party. There was only one blue spoon and one orange spoon, but it seemed worth it. It seemed to be the right thing to do.

The night was still, the shadows unwavering. For a while, Alice imagined playing Sweet or Sour with Mallory and Helen Blair on the streets of the Chinese village.

Her mind wandered. She thought that time passed more slowly at night, especially when you were trying so hard to fall asleep.

She yawned. Tomorrow would be a morning full of good-byes. But now, she realized, was the beginning of the good-byes, because this was the last night. She forced herself to close her eyes.

CHAPTER 21

At the horizon, clouds crammed the sky like rolls of cotton smashed against glass. But up above, the sky was a bright blue bowl. And, under it, Alice, saturated in sunlight, was saying good-bye.

She'd already been down to the ocean and back three times. Once, running as fast as she could. Once, walking and trying to keep her eyes closed as much as possible. And once, listing slightly to one side and then the other, pretending that the wind was shifting.

She'd said good-bye to the sand heart, which wasn't much more than a dimpled hump. She'd said good-bye to the dolphins—wherever they were under the water. She'd said good-bye to the pelicans and the gulls and the sandpipers.

When Alice and her parents walked down to Mr. Barden's cottage to say good-bye to him, he seemed less substantial and extra frail to Alice, as though he'd shrunk overnight. His eyes behind his glasses were watery.

Alice stood taut and stayed right by her father. "See you next year," she said cheerfully, keeping her distance.

"If I'm still alive," Mr. Barden replied.

Alice looked away and let the adults do the rest of the talking.

Then they stopped at the Wishmeiers'. Alice's parents gave the Wishmeiers two bags of groceries, odds and ends they hadn't used. The Wishmeiers gave Alice big, long hugs and a little box filled with chocolates in dark brown, fluted paper cups.

"It won't be the same around here without you," said Mr. Wishmeier.

"Agreed," said Mrs. Wishmeier.

"Thank you for the junonia," said Alice.

Mr. Wishmeier drew in his lips as if he were absorbed in thought. He nodded emphatically. "Thank *you*," he said.

As Alice and her parents walked away, Alice turned and waved until her arm hurt.

Next they said good-bye to the ocean.

Alice sighed so deeply, she felt several inches taller.

"Don't worry," said Alice's father. "It'll be here next year."

"It went so fast," said Alice's mother.

The sun—or the thought of leaving—had made

Alice tired. She wanted to curl up on the beach and nap for a year. It was hard to believe she'd be sleeping in her own bed that night. "Good-bye," she whispered.

Minutes later, in the car, she said good-bye again— to Scallop—and they were on their way to the airport.

When they were driving on the bridge to the mainland, Alice felt the first stirrings of unpleasantness in the pit of her belly. The same feeling she'd experienced on her arrival. But as soon as the feeling rose up, it stopped. Suddenly she felt as if she were the center of everything, like the sun. She was thinking: Here I am. I have my parents. We're alone together. I will never be old. I will never die. It's right now. I'm ten.

KEVIN HENKES is the author of *Sun & Spoon*, *Bird Lake Moon*, and the Newbery Honor Book *Olive's Ocean*. He also writes and illustrates picture books, and among his many titles are the national bestsellers *My Garden*, *Old Bear*, *A Good Day*, and *Kitten's First Full Moon*, for which he was awarded the Caldecott Medal. Mr. Henkes is also the creator of a series of books starring mouse characters, including *Penny and Her Song*, *Lilly's Purple Plastic Purse*, *Lilly's Big Day*, *Wemberly Worried*, *Chrysanthemum,* and *Owen*, for which he was awarded a Caldecott Honor.

Kevin Henkes lives with his family in Madison, Wisconsin.

www.KevinHenkes.com